Thank you for looking at

Book Specifications

Binding: Perfect Binding
Cover: Design Package #1: Cover submitted as film with
   Matchprint®
   Ink: Full color
   Cover Stock: 10 pt.
Text: Typeset by Morris Publishing
   Heading Style: Chapter Heading Style #5
   Chapter Headings: All start on a right-hand page. (With
   this option, it created extra blank pages.)
   Text Font: Palatino
   Text Point Size: 11 point
   Headings: Left: Author Name centered
               Right: Book Title centered
   Page Numbers: Bottom of page & centered
# of Pages: 132 (including this page & 15 blank pages)
Text Paper: Standard Paper -- 50 lb. white
Text Ink: Black
Special Pages: Title Page, Copyright Page, Dedication Page,
   Acknowledgment Page, Table of Contents and Order Form
Special Features: Picture History on pages 101-120

Our commitment t ~~excellence has made us~~
America's #1 short-ru ~~~~ *bud*
to demonstrate the

D1115456

Sample book is for printing sample only.
Not For Resale.

A Light In The Window

by Georgene Pearson

A Light In The Window

Published by: Logos To Rhema Publishing
8210 E. 71st Street #250
Tulsa, OK 74133
(918) 488-9667

Cover: by Bryant Design

ISBN: 1-57502-143-9

Printed in the USA by

MORRIS PUBLISHING

3212 East Highway 30 • Kearney, NE 68847 • 1-800-650-7888

Dedication

For my two children, Linda Lou Godwin and Louis Miller Jr., in loving memory of their grandmother Geneva.

Acknowledgments

This story is dedicated to children who love to read about our American Heritage. It's based on a true story of courageous prairie families in 1930 and 1931.

My special dedication honors Geneva (Miller-Burks-Watson) who is the prairie mother. She provided the newspaper clippings and pictures from the *Denver Post*, Denver, Colorado, *Kiowa County Press*, Eads, Colorado, *Holly Chiefton*, Holly, Colorado, *Kansas City Star*, Kansas City, Missouri, and *The Star Journal*, Pueblo, Colorado. She also provided other keepsake pictures and memorabilia for the story. A special thanks for her memories chapter by chapter.

At the time of this writing Geneva is 91 years old, lives alone and cares for herself. She is the grandmother of my two children, Linda Lou and Louis, Jr.

I also pay tribute to the twenty prairie children in the story who struggled together to survive the most unexpected and life-threatening situation of their lifetime.

Special "Thanks" to Rosemary (Brown) Cannon, Lena (Huffaker) Brock, Alice (Huffaker) Huggins, Laura (Huffaker) Loehr, Blanche (Stonebraker) Widger, and Clara (Smith) Spear who shared their memories of home and the Pleasant Hill School.

Timely information was also given by the late Reverend Archie Nichols. He was pastor of the Assembly of God Church in Holly, Colorado, in 1931. Later, he pastored a church built in memory of the Pleasant Hill children and Carl Miller.

Freda Miller, wife of Ray Miller, was a student at another school nearby. She provided her memories of school and family for the story.

Prices of items purchased at JC Penney Company were provided by JC Penney Archivist, Jerry Probst, Dallas, Texas. Pictures were from Lumar Daily News and Colorado Heritage.

I chose to read my story to the Third and Fourth Grade classes of Mrs. Ellen Vander Berg at the Claremore Christian School in the spring of 1994. Iann Poole and Sarah Farrington won the title contest. They suggested *Tragic Times On The Prairie*. The title was changed by the publisher's request to *A Light In The Window*. The classes selected the chapter titles.

Special gratitude goes to W.O. Randle, Inc., of Holly, Colorado, and Fielding Accent Electric, Collinsville, Oklahoma, for copying materials.

Thanks to Sue Reidel who read the manuscript and believed in my dream for seeing this story in book form.

Last, but not least, my love to my husband Bob, who has encouraged and supported me to write and research. God Bless You!

Table of Contents

1

Moving

The broad flat prairies gave a warm spring welcome to Carl Miller and his family. It was May 1930, the beginning of the depression years. The move seemed to promise a better future here for Carl and Geneva his wife, their seven year old daughter Mary Louise and Louis, their year-and-a-half-old son.

Geneva was a young Oklahoma woman. Even at age twenty-seven she looked more like a small blue-eyed girl than a mother of two. She found the grassy prairie very different from the rolling red hills and booming oil fields south of Oklahoma City.

Carl was a tall thin man, age twenty-nine, eager to be farming and taking care of his cattle. He liked working for himself. Farming would also mean he would be able to spend more time with his family. Carl was not afraid of hard work as he had worked long hard hours in the Oklahoma oil fields and later with a railroad section crew in Kansas.

Mary Louise wasn't exactly what you'd call a tomboy, but she did love the horses, farm animals and the outdoors. She could saddle a horse or harness a team, with the aid of something to stand on, just as good as her daddy. Short brown hair framed her little round face. Bright blue eyes twinkled above her chubby red cheeks and her broad smile revealed straight white teeth.

They were glad to be close to Grandpa and Grandma Miller again. They lived nearby as did Uncle Ray, Uncle Jess and their families.

Carl leased 160 acres; a farm southeast of the small town of Towner, Colorado. There was an adobe house with wood floors for the family. Adobe is mud and grass mixed together to make

1

bricks. These made the house warm in the winter and cool in the summer. The inside and outside were plastered with lime and sand. Before moving from Kansas they had lived in a half dugout, which is something like a basement.

There was also a good barn with a hayloft and wide-board corrals. Some small shedlike buildings nearby could be used for pigs and chickens. Two round corncribs would provide storage for the fall corn crop. A windmill south of the house pumped their water, which they carried to the house. In back of the house was a narrow path that led to the outhouse.

One hundred acres of grassy sod would be pasture for the thirty-head of cows and calves, four horses, and Prince, Mary Louise's spotted Shetland pony. Corn would be planted on the other sixty acres.

Most of the prairie was open range, which meant the cattle grazed everywhere. Barbedwire fences were put around the corn fields to keep the cattle out. At night the cows would be brought in and milked then kept in the corrals or in the barn.

The flat open prairie made it possible to see for miles in every direction. There seemed to be more sky and space than anything else. A few trees grew along a lonely looking creek in the distance. The vast prairie bloomed with colorful wildflowers. Few and far between, small farms dotted the wilderness countryside.

Income for the Miller family would come mostly from selling cream. This money would buy their staple food such as sugar, flour, salt and potatoes. Their chickens and pigs would provide their meat. Geneva would make their lard and soap from the pig fat.

Geneva went right to work getting the house in order. The north room, with the door, would be the storage room and entrance. She needed this space for the milk pails, the cream separator and wash tubs. They'd have some place to hang their coats and leave their barn boots, too. One side of the room would be for storing corncobs for the cookstove and heater, as there was no wood to burn for fuel on the prairie.

The next room would be the kitchen and living area. One piece of furniture was called a kitchen cabinet. It had a flat workspace with cupboards above for dishes; below there was a row of drawers, a bin for flour and a storage place for cooking pans. There was also an iron cookstove and a wood table with four chairs. A small wooden stand with a washbasin and a water bucket sat next to the door. It was a simple little kitchen but Geneva had it sparkling clean and homey in no time.

The two rooms on the west were bedrooms. The smaller room on the north would be the children's bedroom. A half bed, a crib and a small chest with drawers made the room seem even smaller. In the larger room on the south, a bed sat against one wall. A larger chest with drawers sat across the room. Clothes were hung behind a striped curtain in the corner. The heating stove warmed the cozy little room from the other corner.

Curtains would be made of flour sacks or feed sacks sometime later. Kerosene lamps in each room gave the necessary light for the little house.

While Geneva was busy in the house, Carl was getting repairs made on the old sheds as well as the used machinery. He knew it would be planting time in a few weeks and he wanted to be ready.

The spring months passed quickly. Chores took a lot of time. Geneva always helped Carl with the milking both morning and evening. There were also horses, pigs and chickens to feed and eggs to gather.

Mary Louise liked to turn the handle on the cream separator. The milk would be poured into a big steel bowl on the top and when she turned the handle the cream would come out of one spout into a pail and the milk would come out of a different spout into another pail. They poured the cream into a cream can to take to town to sell. Some of the milk would be used by the family and the rest was fed to the pigs.

Mary Louise helped her busy parents by helping with the chores and taking care of her baby brother. She liked playing tag with her little dog, Snowball, and riding her pony, Prince. She'd often say, "I like my daddy and my pony best of all. I like the wide open spaces to ride in and the wind blowing through my hair."

One evening, as the kerosene lamp flickered on the table and Geneva was clearing up the dishes, Carl said, "I met our neighbor John Snow, today. He said school would be starting September 8."

"I knew it was about time," Geneva replied. "Mary Louise will be going to Pleasant Hill School, won't she?"

"Yes, and Mr. Snow said they'd be needing a school bus this year. The school is going to hire someone to bus the students. He asked if I'd be interested in the job. I told him I'd sure check into it," explained Carl.

"That would work out fine with our farm chores and it'd be extra money too," exclaimed Geneva excitedly. "I could get the chores started in the morning while you were picking up the children."

"You're right. You could pick them up after school if I was still in the field, too," Carl answered seriously.

"Oh, I hadn't thought of that," replied Geneva.

"Guess we'd better not make too many plans before I check about it. I'll do that first thing tomorrow. I'll need to know what the requirements are. I think I have to have my own bus. If it pays good enough there would be no problem finding a used school bus."

Mary Louise bounced in just in time to hear the words "school bus" and asked, "Will I get to ride a bus this year?"

"Just maybe," smiled her daddy. "The Pleasant Hill School is planning on having a school bus this year. Your mama and I were just talking about it. I'm going to see more about it tomorrow."

"Your daddy thinks he just might be able to get the job!" said Mama reaching out and taking Mary Louise in her arms giving her a big squeeze.

"Oh! Goody! Goody!" she shouted. "Just think I won't have to worry about being new in this school if my daddy is the bus driver!"

"Now, now I just said I was going to check into it tomorrow. Don't count your chickens before they're hatched," laughed her daddy.

"I'll be in the third grade this year," she informed both her parents as she stretched herself as tall as she could.

Her mother reminded her, "You'll be going to Pleasant Hill just west of here. It's the school where the Baker's took you to Sunday School."

"Oh, yes, there are two schoolhouses there. I wonder which one I'll be going to?" she asked.

"We'll just have to check that out," answered her mama as she picked up the baby. "It's time for your bath and bedtime, little boy."

The little prairie family continued to talk about their hopes and plans for the future until the kerosene lamp flickered out.

Georgene Pearson

chapter

2

New Job

The School Board meeting was held on the first Monday night in July. Carl was there to find out more about the plans for a bus and a driver. After some discussion to work out the details, the school approved Carl's application for the job.

He was very busy the next few weeks finding a good used bus, getting it ready for the first day of school, and keeping the farm chores done. He had bought a 1929 Chevrolet truck with a wood bus body. It had five windows on each side. Inside were two long wooden benches below the windows. There was a small aisle down the middle, an emergency door in the back, and a door in the front for the student et on the bus. There was just enough ro~~m~~ ents who would be riding this year.

School would be ~~number~~ 8, right after Labor Day. The Miller family was excited. Carl was glad to have the extra job. Geneva was happy to know there would be fifty dollars more for the family expenses their first winter in Colorado. Mary Louise was excited that her daddy would be the new bus driver. They could hardly wait for school to begin.

"I'm going for a practice drive today," announced Carl after breakfast one morning. "I have the list of all the students and – just who would like to go along for the ride?"

"Me! Me!" shouted Mary Louise. After all it had seemed as if Daddy had been working on that bus for ages. She was eager to know where all the kids lived, too.

"I thought you just might like to ride along. Mama and Louis may want to come with us too," he said to Mary Louise. "Mama will need to know the bus route if she's going to pick the kids up sometimes."

"Just give me a minute to clear up these dishes and we can be on our way. I'm sure both of the kids will enjoy the ride," replied Geneva.

"I'll take care of the dishes, Mama," Mary Louise said as she started gathering up the plates. She was sure anxious to get her first ride on the bus.

"Just put them in the dish pan on the cabinet, dear, and I'll get Louis dressed," answered her mama. Geneva couldn't help but think what a big help her little girl had been all summer. She was sure going to miss her when school started. She knew she had enjoyed riding Prince, her pony. "I believe that girl would rather ride than eat when she's hungry," thought Geneva. "I'll be there in a minute," she called from the bedroom. "You can go on out to the bus with Daddy."

She raced out through the storage room to find her daddy already in the bus. As she ran up to the bus he opened the door. "Welcome aboard, little lady," he chuckled. "Guess you're ready for school today!"

"Oh, Daddy, this is not a school day."

"I just thought we'd pretend," he teased as he patted her on the head.

Soon Geneva came out of the house carrying Louis. He was excited too. He was going for a ride.

"Wide! Wide!" he was saying as he was just learning to talk. Geneva set him down on the first step and his sister helped him on up into the bus and up on the bench behind their daddy.

"Everyone ready?" asked Carl as he turned the key on.

"Ready, Daddy! Ready!" she squealed excitedly. So, Carl got out and went around to the front of the bus and pulled up on the crank. The motor chugged to a start on the very first pull.

"How's that?" asked Carl as he climbed back into the driver's seat.

"That's great," said Geneva proudly. She had a lot of respect for her husband's mechanical skills. He had always been able to keep their cars, tractors and farm machinery running. They had never been able to buy new equipment. Times were very hard and no one had much money to buy anything.

Carl shifted the bus into gear and they were off. Everyone was excited even if the ride was bumpy as they bounced along the country road.

Carl told them about each family and farm on the route. The first bus stop would be at the Black's. He would pick up three children there. There would be six children to pick up at the Huff's place. They had a big two-story adobe house. Part of the house was a dugout with another house beside it, but they were hooked together. The next stop would be at the Snow's and there were two children there. As he checked the list, they went on to a larger farm and it was a very pretty place. He would pick up the two Baker girls there, then across the prairie road to the Jones' to pick up one boy, Jimmy.

"Oh! we're already back to our farm, Daddy!" Mary Louise said in surprise.

"Yes, if you aren't ready to go when I leave, now will be the time you will get on the bus," explained her daddy. We still have to pick up more children, though."

As they continued on Carl explained that the next stop would be the Teague's farm, he'd have four children there. The last stop would be to pick up one girl at the Smithover's and then on to the schoolhouse, which was one mile south.

"This is the way we'll go every day," Carl said as they pulled up at the school gate. Right now the gate was locked and the schoolhouses were empty, but that would change very soon.

"I wonder what it will be like going to school here?" thought Mary Louise aloud as she looked around the school grounds.

"I imagine you will have a very good time, dear, and you'll make a lot of new friends."

They had laughed and talked as they went from farm to farm. Now Carl turned the bus around and they started home, which was a mile and a half east of the school. It had been lots of fun looking out across the prairie on a calm day like today. The huge sky seemed such a pale blue compared to the bright yellow glow of the sun. Not every day was like this for if the wind was blowing hard the sky would be dark and gray with sand and dirt.

"When will school start?" asked Mary Louise, as she was getting anxious. She knew Daddy had told her, but she really wanted to know just how many more days were left.

"September eighth, just two more weeks," answered her mama. "The time will go fast, it'll be here before you know it."

"I have good feelings and bad feelings about starting school." Mary Louise had said her thoughts out loud. "I've had so much fun here on the farm I really hate for it to end."

"Just think about the good feelings that you will have being home on Saturdays, Sundays and holidays," encouraged Mama.

"You'll make a lot of new friends, too," added her daddy. "I think you'll like your new teacher, Miss Emory. I hear she is a very good teacher."

"I sure hope so," she answered slowly. She was thinking about Miss Andrews, her second grade teacher. She really did like her a lot. She was also wondering if the school would be different here in Colorado than it was in Kansas, where she had gone to school last year.

"Will I get to be the first one on the bus?" she asked.

"Some mornings you may want to be first and then there may be sometimes I can pick you up on my way back if you're not ready to go. I'll leave kinda early you know, about seven o'clock."

By now Louis was asleep and Geneva just enjoyed looking around and being away from the farm for a while. There was always so much work to be done.

As they pulled up into their yard, Carl turned the motor off and said, "This extra job will sure help us get through the winter."

"We couldn't ask for anything better, could we? It seems almost too good to be true. We haven't been here very long. It's a wonder the school board didn't hire someone who had lived here longer," commented Geneva.

Carl was shaking his head in agreement. "Guess it's time to get back to work. I need to work on that corn trailer. It'll soon be corn picking time and I sure want that floor fixed. I don't want to lose any corn between the field and the corncrib," replied Carl.

Mary Louise knew what she was going to do, that is, if Mama didn't need her for a while. She'd saddle Prince and go for a ride since she wouldn't have many more days to be alone with her pony.

She really needed to tell him all about the bus, her school, and just how much she was going to miss him.

Geneva said, "I've got some sewing to do. Since Louis will be sleeping for a while – maybe I could get some of it finished before dinner."

That's just what Mary Louise wanted to hear, Mother would be doing something that didn't need her help. "May I saddle Prince and go for a ride?" she asked.

"I don't see why not," her mama answered. "Be back by dinner. That's when the sun is straight up and you can't see your shadow."

With that she was off to the barn to saddle her faithful friend, Prince. "You want to go for a ride, ole pal?" she asked. He only nickered and nuzzled his little mistress, but she understood his noisy answer as he rubbed his nose against her back.

3

Back To School

The first day of school finally arrived. It was a beautiful fresh morning under the never-ending blue sky.

"I want to go with you when you leave this morning," announced Mary Louise as they were finishing breakfast.

"That will be fine with me," answered her daddy. "I can introduce you and myself as the kids get on the bus."

"I can hardly wait," she answered excitedly. She was wearing the new blue printed dress her mama had just finished. Her hair was neatly brushed and a blue ribbon was tied in her dark brown hair. She did have to wear her only pair brown shoes, which were really scuffed. Mama ~~SAMPLE BOOK~~ lish on them which did help their looks. ~~Not For Resale~~ hing made her blue eyes twinkle and a b ~~across~~ her shiny face.

"I'll take Louis w ~~me~~ to the barn and start the milking," Geneva said to Carl.

"You have a good day, Sweetie, and we'll see you after school," she said to Mary Louise as she leaned down and gave her a little peck on the cheek. "And don't forget your lunch bucket, now."

Mary Louise had watched her mama pack a jelly sandwich and a piece of chocolate cake in the empty syrup bucket. She knew she would be hungry by noon. Mama's chocolate cake was always a special treat.

As Carl and Mary Louise left on the bus, Mama and Louis were waving goodbye – then they went on to the barn to start the milking. Carl would be back before very long. Louis always liked to play in the barn. Snowball was usually there too, and he liked playing with the dog.

Carl stopped to pick up the first three children at the Black's farm. There were two girls older than Mary Louise and one boy younger. As Carl opened the door he said, "Good morning, children. Just find a seat, then let's find out your names." The children quickly found a seat and Carl introduced himself, "I'm Carl Miller, you may call me Carl and this is my daughter, Mary Louise. Now, what shall we call you?"

"I'm Rose," spoke up the older girl. "This is my sister, Mabel and my brother, Roland."

"So glad to meet you all. I'll be your bus driver this year," he said as he closed the bus door. The girls began to chat right away but Roland just stared out the window. That didn't last long for there were six children at the next stop. Now there were ten excited boys and girls. The bus was new to all of them so they were excited about the ride as well as it being the first day of school.

An older girl and a younger boy got on when the bus stopped at the Snow's. Carl greeted all the children with the same cheerful greeting. They in turn would tell him their names and find a place to sit. The Snow's and the Huff's were cousins and they were happy to be spending more time together.

At the Baker's they picked up two older girls. Mary Louise had gone to Sunday School with them at the schoolhouse so she already knew May and Brenda. At the next stop they picked up the Jones' boy whose name was Jimmy. This was his first year in school and he didn't have any brothers or sisters. He did know Larry Snow who was his age.

When the bus went by the Miller's farm, Carl pointed it out to the kids. "This is where we live, boys and girls." Everyone turned to look as they passed so they'd remember next time. They continued on to pick up the Teague children. There were three boys and one girl, Erlene. She was about Mary Louise's age.

The last stop was at the Smithover's. One older girl, Crissie, got on there. She went back to sit with Rose Black and Alicia Huff, the older girls she knew.

Now all twenty students were anxiously awaiting their arrival at school. There was lots of laughing and talking as they drove the last mile south to the school. Most of the children hadn't seen each other all summer. When Carl drove the bus into the schoolyard the children gathered up their lunch pails from under the bench. They were ready to get out as soon as he opened the bus door. Another bus from west of the school was unloading too.

"See you after school," Carl was saying to all the children as they stepped off the bus. Mary Louise waited until last to get off. She wanted to give her daddy a hug and say, "Good-bye."

Carl took the cream can of water to the schoolhouse. There was no water well there so the school board had asked Carl to take water every day for Miss Emory's students.

"Good morning Miss Emory, I'm Carl Miller, the new bus driver," greeted Carl as he took off his hat.

"So glad to meet you Mr. Miller, and I do hope that all went well for you this first morning," answered Miss Emory standing outside the schoolhouse.

"Everything was fine, thank you. I have a daughter, Mary Louise, who will be in your third-grade class this year. You'll be meeting her after a while."

"I'm glad to know that and I'm sure we will have a good year."

"Just where would you want me to put the water, Miss Emory?"

"Oh, right there on the stand just inside the door," she answered pointing inside.

Carl stepped inside and lifted the cream can up on the wooden stand. A tin cup was already hanging from a round rod above the stand. A washbasin was sitting there. A feedsack towel hung on the side. It would soon be time for the bell so Carl wished Miss Emory a good day and returned to his bus. The other bus driver came over and introduced himself.

"I'm Don Johnson. I'm bringing children west of here," he stated.

"I'm Carl Miller, glad to meet you Mr. Johnson," answered Carl. They chatted briefly. They found out that both of them had chores to finish up so they didn't tarry very long.

As the schoolbell rang the children scurried into the school-houses. The older children, in the eighth and ninth grades, were together. Mr. Fry was the teacher. All the students in first through seventh grades went to Miss Emory's building.

As the children were filing in, Miss Emory was saying, "Good morning, boys and girls, you may put your lunch pails on the shelf at the back of the room." When the last child was in she came on into the room. "Please find a desk and be seated for now." Then Miss Emory walked up to the front of the room and rang a small bell on her desk to get the children's attention.

"Hello boys and girls," said Miss Emory again with a smile. "Welcome to Pleasant Hill School. I'm Miss Emory." Then she walked to the chalkboard and printed her name, M-i-s-s E-m-o-r-y. She turned around and said, "Will you please stand for the opening exercises." Everyone stood beside their desk and followed Miss Emory in the Pledge of Allegiance. Then she sang one verse of America and bowed her head and said the Lord's Prayer. The children who knew all the words followed along. Mary Louise was thinking, "This was what they had done in school in Kansas." It sure made her feel good as she remembered all the words.

Miss Emory was tall and looked kind of thin. She had dark brown hair done up in a bun. Her soft brown eyes, short nose and thin lips made her a pretty lady. She had a soft voice so everyone had to listen and pay attention. Most of all she was cheerful and kind.

"You may be seated. I have a list of all your names and the grades you are starting. Well arrange our seating according to grades," she continued. "But first let's get acquainted. I would like you to tell me your name and something you enjoyed doing this summer."

Right away Mary Louise thought, "This is going to be easy" – she would forget about being nervous when she talked about her pony, Prince.

After getting acquainted Miss Emory said, "Now we will sort of have fruit basket upset. I want all the students in first grade to choose a seat in the front row, now the second grade students will be next, then we'll have third, fourth and fifth, then sixth and seventh take the seats at the back." The students moved as directed without much difficulty.

"Now, if you have chosen a seat where you do not work well, I will have to move you later," she warned the children. There were eighteen students all together.

Next, she pointed out the assignment sections already printed on the chalkboard except for the first grade. She explained that she would be helping them.

"Boys and girls, we'll begin these assignments after a fifteen minute recess," announced Miss Emory.

The children were all glad for a chance to be outside again as it was getting warm in the school. At least there was a little breeze outside. The boys went right to their ball game, but the girls were looking for some shade near the building.

It seemed to Mary Louise that time was flying. After recess the older children began to work on the assignments that were on the chalkboard for spelling and math. Miss Emory was helping the first-graders to print their names. Then they did some alphabet drills, too. Soon Miss Emory said, "Boys and girls you may put your finished assignments on my desk. If you have any unfinished work you may complete it after lunch."

Then she instructed the children about the lunch hour. Everyone was to wash their hands. They could eat inside or out but they must finish their lunch before playing. They were also to go to the outhouse before classes began again.

When the children were ready to play, Miss Emory had also finished her lunch. She went outside to watch the children. She got the girls playing Drop the Handkerchief while the boys were playing ball. Miss Emory rang the bell to let the children know that the lunch hour was over. They all lined up noisily at the door. She rang the bell again for them to be quiet; then everyone filed inside to their seats.

The afternoon went by quickly; the students finished the assignments. Some had time to color or do some reading from the library shelf.

Mary Louise knew that she already liked the new school and the teacher. Miss Emory had colorful pictures on the walls and there were extra books to read and check out. She also had some games and puzzles. Some green plants were set by the windows. Mary Louise was glad she would be coming back tomorrow.

Miss Emory interrupted her thoughts by announcing it was time to get ready to go home. "I would like for today's helpers to stack the reading chairs and empty the trash. We will have two volunteers to erase the chalkboard and straighten up our book shelf." The classroom was a bustle in no time. In a few minutes everything was in order. "Since you've cleaned up so quickly we'll have time to start a story," Miss Emory said proudly. She took a book from her desk and sat down on a tall stool by her desk.

"The name of this book is *The Wonderful Wizard of Oz*. The author is Frank L. Baum," she said as she showed the students the colorful cover of the book; then she opened the book and began to read. She read for a short while then marked her place and closed the book. "That's all for this time, we'll have to begin here tomorrow as it is time to go home." Some low murmuring made her know the children were going to enjoy her reading to them.

Miss Emory laid the book on her desk and said, "Please stand. We'll file out one row at a time, beginning with row one. Please follow me." Then she led the students out.

Both buses were parked and ready for the students to get on. As Mary Louise got on the bus she hugged her daddy and said, "We had such a good time today, Daddy."

"I sure am glad to hear that, little lady," Carl answered with a twinkle in his eyes and a smile on his face. "Your mama will be happy to hear that too."

Carl greeted all the students as they stepped into the bus again. He then remembered he had to pick up the cream can. It took him just a little while to go after it. Carl cranked the engine and got on the bus. They were soon on their way home. The weary children were much quieter for the warm ride home.

Carl opened and closed the bus door at the Black's farm for the last three children to get off.

"See you tomorrow," he repeated again. Mary Louise moved up to sit right behind her daddy for the rest of the ride to their home.

"I sure am hungry, Daddy."

"Mama will have a snack ready as soon as we get home, then we've got a surprise," he said teasingly.

"Surprise!" exclaimed Mary Louise forgetting all about being hungry. "Oh! tell me, Daddy, pleeese," she begged.

Georgene Pearson

4

Surprises

Mama and Louis were waiting at the door when Carl drove the bus up in the yard. Mary Louise dashed to the house excited about the surprise.

"We got a prize," her brother was saying. "We got a prize."

"I know! I know! What is the surprise?" she asked squatting down so she could look him in the eyes.

"No tell, can't tell," was his smiling, teasing answer.

Geneva and Carl were both very proud that Louis hadn't given the secret away. "I know you're excited but you've got to change your clothes first," encouraged her mama.

"Oh! It must be a new baby ~~~~," she guessed. She knew the barn cat was ~~~~ some baby calves were also about due ~~~~

"Now, I thought ~~~~ you were hungry, little lady," taunted her daddy. "Get your clothes changed; then well have some of Mama's warm cookies and then we can go to the barn."

Louis followed her to the bedroom saying, "Hurry up – you want to see the prize?"

"Of course! But I have to change my clothes first." He really had missed her today. He was happy she was home again. "I 'elp' Mama bake cookie for you. Want some?"

"Sure, I want some of your cookies," she was saying to him as she put on her old shoes and socks. "Let's go, I'm ready now."

They went back to the kitchen where Mama and Daddy were already sitting at the table. A plate of sugar cookies was already on the table and four glasses of milk. The smell of warm cookies just out of the oven did remind her that she was hungry.

The surprise at the barn would just have to wait. As they ate the cookies and drank the milk, Mary Louise chatted about the big day at school. She didn't want to take time now to tell it all – some of the details could wait until later. "I'm finished. Let's go to the barn now."

Mama picked up the empty plate and the glasses and put them in the dish pan. They all headed for the barn. Mary Louise ran on ahead and Louis was coming as fast as his short legs would take him.

"I'm going to check on the barn cat first," she thought. She stopped suddenly when she walked through the door for there sat Blackie on top of the manger. "It's not Blackie," she called to her folks. "What is it, Daddy?"

"Well, let's go!" he said as he reached out and took her by the hand. Daddy led her through the barn to a stall on the other side. She peeked through the boards in the gate so she could see.

"Oh my!" she squealed, "Molly had twins!"

"Prize! Prize!" yelled Louis as he toddled up beside her.

Sure enough, there were two little calves that looked exactly alike. Molly was the tamest cow they had. She really was a pet.

"Can we pet 'em?" she asked turning around to her daddy.

"Sure, just a minute though. I'll have to let Molly out first; then you and Louis can go in and pet the little heifers."

She knew why Daddy had said that, Mama cows can be mean when they have babies to protect. The kids stepped out of the way and in just a little bit Daddy had Molly out in the corral. Now they could go into the stall and pet the calves.

The calves were snuggled down in the bed of fresh straw. Mama and Daddy stood there and watched the children pet the new calves. They "oooood" and "aaaad" and checked them out from nose to tail. They were little Jersey calves so they looked like little deer. They were a light chocolate color with black noses and real soft black eyes. The insides of their ears were pink. Their fur was soft and fuzzy.

"Guess you'll have to decide on their names," suggested Mama. "Can you tell them apart?" she quizzed.

By now the little calves were standing up on their four wobbly legs. Right away Mary Louise could tell one of them was bigger than the other. "This one is bigger, Mama," she said as she pointed to the larger one.

"You're right, but when they grow some they may be the same size," reminded her Mama.

"I guess we could put different colored bells on them," she laughed.

In the meantime while the children were occupied with the calves, Carl had gone to bring the cows in. Sometimes they would come in on their own and sometimes Carl would have to ride out on the prairie and drive them in. Tonight he'd saddle Zipper. When Mary Louise went after them she always rode Prince.

Mama finally decided that she would get the hay out for the cows and put the feed in the manger so they'd be ready to milk when Carl got back. The children stayed in the stall with the twins trying to decide on their names. They had to be special, just right, for these were the first twins born on their farm.

Louis was standing by the babies making a humming sound like "Meh-eh-eh."

"Their names must begin with 'M' like Molly's" she thought. "I know Louis, we can call them Mandy and Mindy! 'A' comes first in the alphabet, so well name the biggest one Mandy and the smaller one Mindy."

"Mindy! Mindy!" Louis repeated.

"No, Mandy and Mindy!" she exclaimed. "Oh, well!" She knew the difference. "Come on, let's go tell Mama and Daddy."

So they left the stall, making sure the gate was shut. She thought Mama and Daddy would like the names she had picked.

By this time Carl and Geneva had already started to milk. You could hear the 'ping, ping, ping' as the streams of warm milk hit the bottom of the pails. When the pails were full and ready to empty into the cream can, Mary Louise knew her parents could hear her so she said, "I decided Mandy and Mindy would be two good names."

"I like those names, don't you Carl?"

"Sure do – they begin just like Molly," her daddy commented, then went right on back to the milking.

"Why don't you and Louis go to the henhouse and gather the eggs? Take them on to the house. We'll be finished here in a little while – then you can turn the handle on the separator," suggested Mama.

"May we take another look at the baby calves first?" she asked.

"Of course, but don't open the gate this time," Mama advised.

So the two of them went back to the stall to take another peek at the babies. They had already lain down in the straw with their eyes closed. "Aren't they cute, Louis?" Mary Louise asked as the two of them were looking between the boards. He just nodded his head and grinned from ear to ear.

The kids gathered the eggs, much to the dislike of the chickens. "Guess they don't like for us to disturb them," she thought for they jumped around and squawked a lot. Louis thought all the commotion was funny as he was enjoying the noise and all the flying feathers.

When they got to the house Mary Louise put the eggs in the egg crate. Shortly, Mama and Daddy came from the barn with the milk. Mama got the separator ready and Daddy poured the milk in the big bowl on top, then Mary Louise began to turn the handle. She liked to watch the milk and cream come out different spouts.

Mama went to get a pitcher so she could have some fresh milk before it was all separated. When they were finished, Daddy poured the cream into the cream can and took the milk to the pigs.

Mama had started supper so in a little while everyone was washed up and ready to eat. As the little family sat down to supper that night they had lots to talk about. There was time now to talk about school, the kids, the teacher, the bus ride, and yes, of course, the new additions to the farm – Molly's new twins Mandy and Mindy.

chapter

5

Entertainment

The fall days of September were busy getting the bus schedule worked in with the morning and evening chores. Carl had also started the corn picking. His brother helped him. They helped each other with their crops, so they would be extra busy for the next few weeks.

Geneva drove the bus to pick the students up after school. Louis was excited about going on the bus.

"Wide da bus!" he would say when they left in the evening. He always enjoyed seeing the children getting on and off the bus, especially his sister.

Geneva and Mary Louise would do the chores as soon as they got home. Mary Louise would saddle Prince and ride out after the cows. She'd love to ride across the prairie pastures – the wind blowing through her short brown hair. She could ride as well as Mama or Daddy. This was her chance to tell Prince all about what was going on at school. She knew he missed her and would really want to know.

Carl would usually be in from the field before chores were done so he'd put the hay out for the cows and horses and feed the pigs.

The family had time together while they ate supper. They could talk about what had happened during the day and what was planned for tomorrow. Mary Louise would help clear the table and either wash or dry the dishes. Then she'd begin her homework by the lamplight. Mama and Daddy would have some time to play with Louis before the day ended.

The October mornings came quickly and it was now much cooler. You really had to wear a coat but it would warm up during the day. The wind seemed to be sweeping a fresh path across the prairie every day. Carl thought the corn picking would be done by the last of the month.

October was also when the school planned to start the box suppers to raise money for books and supplies. It was a good time for neighbors to get together, too. Each family brought a dinner in a decorated box then it would be 'auctioned off' to the highest bidder. The most fun was when the girls brought a 'dinner for two' and hoped some special boy would buy their box and eat with them.

After the dinner there would be games for everyone. One of everyone's favorite was the cake walk. The ladies always made beautiful cakes.

Other entertainment in the area was the barn dances held on the weekends. Living eighteen miles from town made local entertainment much more important to the prairie farmer and his family. It was just too costly to travel that far.

Geneva and Carl both liked to dance so they were anxious to get started. The dances were always canceled during the summer months and then would begin again in the fall. The dances were for the whole family and Mary Louise liked to dance too.

Local farmers were the musicians – fiddle players, guitar pickers and harmonica players. They also did the square dance calling.

A costume dance was planned at the Hill's barn for Halloween, which was on a Friday this year. The Millers knew they could attend as Saturday was not a school day and the corn picking would be done by then.

Mama had suggested that they all be a Hobo family as she didn't have much time to make costumes. Mary Louise gave her enthusiastic answer, "I could wear Daddy's overalls and shirt, couldn't I?"

"I thought so, and so could I," answered her mama.

"We could fix Louis up in some of your clothes, too."

"Guess we'll have to borrow a pair of Grandpa's overalls for Daddy," laughed Mary Louise.

"That won't be a problem, I bet Mama already had that figured out," declared Carl.

There seemed to be lots going on this time of the year. Miss Emory was keeping the children busy. She had the students writing Halloween stories and doing art. The classroom looked alive with orange jack-o-lanterns, black cats and white ghosts. She had told the children they would plan a Halloween party for Friday the thirty-first. This would be the first classroom party for the year.

When Carl picked the children up after the Halloween party they were still excited. Some of the children were going with their families to the Halloween barn dance. They did a lot of talking about costumes on that ride home.

As Carl dropped off the last three children at the Black's farm he said to Mary Louise, "We're going to do the chores right away when we get home. In fact, Mama probably has already gone after the cows, so change your clothes and go straight to the barn."

"OK, Daddy, I'll hurry." She was gathering up her books and lunch pail as she spoke.

Carl parked the bus at the back door and opened the door. Right away Mary Louise was out and headed to the house. "See ya in a minute," she yelled over her shoulder.

No time was wasted doing the chores. The cows were milked, calves and horses were fed, hay was put in the mangers, eggs were gathered.

"We might need to eat a bite before we go," Geneva was telling Carl as they finished separating the milk. "I know we're having a potluck supper but it may be awhile before they eat." She was really thinking about the children.

Mama had sent Mary Louise and Louis on in to get dressed when they came back to the house. Carl agreed. "Yes, and I'm a tad hungry myself."

Mama stepped up to the kitchen door and called, "Oh, Mary Louise?"

"Yes, Mama?" she answered.

"Would you set some small plates and milk glasses on the table, we'll eat a bite before we leave," Mama said.

"Good, cause I'm hungry now. I have Louis dressed in my overalls and shirt. He just has to put on my hat and his shoes. His clothes are baggy all right."

As soon as Mama was finished in the storage room, she came into the kitchen washed the separator parts and the milk pails while Carl took the milk out to feed the pigs.

Mama sliced some fresh bread and put out some homemade butter and jelly. She filled all the glasses with cold milk. When Carl got back she called the kids to come and eat.

"Looks like we have two little bums eating with us tonight," Carl laughed.

"Oh, Daddy, this is just pretend. We're not really bums," reminded Mary Louise.

"But it's fun to pretend, isn't it?" asked Mama.

"You are two cute little bums, if I may say so myself."

"I bum! I bum!" repeated Louis with bread and jelly in his mouth.

They all laughed, too, as he had jelly on both sides of his mouth. When they were all finished Mary Louise picked up the dishes and put them in the dish pan. She put away the bread, butter and jelly that was left. Then she washed and dried the few dishes to surprise Mama.

In the meantime, Mama and Daddy were getting cleaned up and dressed in their hobo outfits. Mama did have some red material so everyone had a red scarf to wear around his neck. Now the Hobo Family was ready for an evening of fun!

As they drove to the Hill's barn they laughed and talked. They were having such a good time – meeting new people, making new friends, plenty of corn for the cattle and some extra money from the bus route for the family. They could relax tonight and enjoy the dance without a worry.

chapter

Shopping

The families on the prairie were enjoying a break from all the spring and summer work. Now it was time to get ready for the long winter months ahead. The weather was changing fast. They'd already had some low temperatures and a light frost. The days were getting shorter and the prairie winds made it seem even colder now. Winter was just around the corner!

Geneva suggested, "We need to plan to go shopping when we take the cream to Holly. We need to get the children winter coats, overshoes, socks and long johns."

"We should do that before Thanksgiving. I've heard the weather changes fast out here by the first of December," warned Carl. "You and the kids need to go."

Mary Louise heard part of the conversation about getting coats. "Are we going to get new coats?"

"Daddy and I were just saying that we need to do some shopping for some winter clothes including winter coats. Would you like to have a new coat?" asked Mama.

"Oh, yes, Mama, that would make me so happy!" was her delighted reply. "When will we go?"

Mama checked the calendar and it was decided they'd go on Saturday the fifteenth. They could eat an early dinner then drive to Holly. They'd have plenty of time to shop. They would take the cream to the creamery on Cheyenne Street first and get the groceries last.

Usually when they took the cream to Holly they only had enough money to buy groceries at IGA. They didn't have to buy much just flour, sugar, salt, baking powder, and soda. They had meat, eggs, milk, butter and lard.

The Miller families had shared extra vegetables from their gardens so Geneva had some homecanned foods for the winter. Next spring they would be able to have a garden of their own.

Geneva had been saving money from the new bus job. She knew they would be needing warmer clothes for the winter here in Colorado.

Saturday the fifteenth finally arrived. The milking was done about the time the sun was coming up. "Sure looks like a beautiful day to go to town," remarked Geneva as they headed back to the house with the milk. "I'm glad the weather isn't bad yet."

"I don't imagine we'll have many good days left, though," stated Carl matter-of-factly. "I'll have to go back to the barn to check on Sally. She should have her calf in a couple of hours or so."

"I'll go ahead and get the kids up and we'll eat breakfast, then we can finish up the chores." Geneva could always manage her time well so she got lots of work done in a short time.

The children were delighted when they woke up and Mama was saying "Arise and shine! Today we're going shopping, remember?"

After waking up, Mary Louise inquired, "What dress can I wear, Mama?"

"One of your nice school dresses will be fine, but I want you to wait until after breakfast to dress. Daddy and I still need to finish some chores and you can dress then."

A quick, light breakfast of oatmeal, fresh bread, butter and jelly was soon on the table and eaten. "I'll wash the dishes," volunteered Mary Louise as she was picking up her bowl and glass.

"That will sure help, then Daddy and I can get the feeding and haying done."

The next couple of hours seemed to drag for Mary Louise but she understood that all the animals had to be taken care of before they could leave.

After she'd finished the dishes and dressed, she sat down with Louis and read him some stories. He liked to look at the pictures and listen to his sister read.

It was after ten o'clock before Carl and Geneva were finished with the chores and back to the house.

"We got another little heifer calf. She's doing fine," Carl was telling the children because he knew they were always excited about the new babies. "It's Sally this time."

"Daddy, can we go see?" asked Mary Louise as she jumped up and ran to her daddy.

"I don't think so just now. The baby was just born a little while ago so you'd better wait until we do chores tonight," advised her daddy as he reached out and patted her on the head.

"May I choose a name for her?" questioned Mary Louise.

"Of course, you'll have all day to be thinking about a name. It's Sally's calf and it looks a lot like Molly's twins," informed her daddy.

"You sure have this kitchen tidy, Sweetheart. You are so helpful," Mama boasted as she put her arms around her little daughter and gave her a big squeeze.

"I like to do it, Mama."

Carl and Geneva cleaned up and dressed to go to town. Carl went out to put the cream can in the car and check on some medicine he needed while Geneva fixed a light lunch. They'd be home in time to have a snack before chore time.

The first stop was to take the cream to the creamery. There were several stores where they could buy clothes – White's Dry Goods, Apples Men's Clothing Store or at the JC Penney Company store. Geneva suggested they try JC Penney Company first. They always had good merchandise and fair prices.

They went to the children's department first. After trying on several coats Mary Louise found one she liked. "I really like this blue one. May I get this coat?" she asked with a big smile across her face.

"That's the one I like best too," was Geneva's comment as she continued to look it over to make sure it fit. "It's a good price too, $2.98."

"What do you think, Daddy?" Mary Louise asked.

"Now, Sweetie, you're the one who is going to wear the coat so you choose what you like," he said seriously. "It is pretty," Daddy agreed.

Now it was time to choose a coat for Louis. Mary Louise was eager to help choose one for him too. A brown tweed one fit just perfect and made him look like a little man. It wasn't hard to decide when they all liked the same one. The coat was the same price, only $2.98. Of course, Louis liked them all and wanted them all!

Next they went to the shoe department to look for some overshoes. They had brown and black ones. Mary Louise wanted black so they found a pair her size. Then a smaller brown pair for Louis. They were forty-nine cents a pair. Geneva also looked at the price of shoes. They were $2.79 a pair. They would have to get shoes later. The children both needed hats and gloves. Mary Louise chose a pair of red gloves and a red and blue stocking cap. Geneva chose a brown hat with ear flaps that fastened over the top for Louis and a pair of brown mittens. These items were less than $2.00. She also selected two pairs of long brown stockings for nineteen cents a pair and two pairs of long johns for twenty-nine cents each for Mary Louise. She'd need these to help stay warm at school.

Now that the shopping was finished for the children, Carl suggested, "You need to look for a coat for yourself. The children and I will take these packages to the car while you look."

So Geneva went to the ladies department. Right away she found a blue coat that she liked very much. It was a perfect fit. She checked the price tag. It was fourteen dollars and seventy-five cents, which was a good price. "I'll wait until Carl returns to decide for sure," she thought to herself. She didn't have a winter coat so she really did need one. She had been saving some of the cream check money all summer for a coat.

Geneva browsed through the store. There were just so many nice things she just enjoyed looking. Some soft pink and blue striped gingham was only ten cents a yard. It would take less than three yards to make a dress. The ready-made dresses sold for seventy-nine cents. She could get material later, she was thinking when Carl and the children returned.

"That is really pretty, Mama," Mary Louise said as she stood beside Geneva.

"It would make a beautiful dress," agreed Geneva.

"Right now we'll check on a coat I found," she said as she led the way to see if Carl approved of her choice.

Geneva tried the coat on again. "It looks fine to me if it's the one you like," was Carl's manly comment.

"OK, I'll take it," she told the clerk who put it in a box and tied a string around it.

"Now, we need to look for Daddy a coat," said Geneva looking around for the men's section. Carl needed a warm coat to wear on the bus. He tried on several and decided on a brown wool mackinaw coat that cost three dollars and ninety-eight cents. They also decided on a pair of Pay Day overalls as they were only seventy-nine cents. "You need some gloves too," reminded Geneva.

"I like to get my gloves over at Romer's Mercantile. I have to stop there today anyway," answered Carl.

"Good, the children and I can look around there too," answered Geneva as she helped Carl take off the coat. The clerk put the coat and overalls in a big sack and they were ready to leave.

As they left the store Geneva looked up the street, "I'd like to stop at White's Dry Goods. I just want to look around."

"That's fine," said Carl, "we have time. Mary Louise can go with you and I'll take Louis with me and go over to Manning's Hardware. Well meet you at IGA in about thirty minutes."

It was a real treat to have time to just look around. The time seemed to go fast. There were just so many nice things. "Times will be better next year," she told herself.

They carefully selected the groceries that were on the list and put them in the car, then they drove down by the railroad tracks to Romer's Mercantile. Everyone got out to look around as Carl selected his gloves and bought some purple medicine for the horses and cows. When Mary Louise saw the bottle she knew what Daddy used it for. It was for cuts or sores.

"It must burn, too," she thought for the animals really did kick when Daddy used it.

As they were leaving the store Carl said, "I believe we have enough time and money to buy some ice cream cones." It only cost five cents a dip.

"Really, Daddy! Can we choose any flavor?" asked Mary Louise reaching out and getting her daddy by the hand.

"Cream! I cream!" Louis squealed jumping up and down and clapping his hands. He knew what ice cream was, that's for sure!

So, they drove down to Bean's Drug Store. It took a little while to make up their minds. This was a special treat. Mary Louise had chocolate, Louis wanted the red kind, and Carl and Geneva both had strawberry.

"Looks like well have to eat our ice cream on the way home," said Geneva looking up at the clock. "It'll be chore time when we get home."

After the ice cream was finished the children dozed off to sleep as the little car rocked back and forth on the rough country road. "The kids sure had a good time, didn't they?" asked Geneva as she looked at her husband.

"They really did. I just wish we could do this more often," answered Carl as he glanced over to Geneva. "I'm sure the farm will do better next year. We can always have hope for another year."

"We can't complain, 1930 has been a good year for us," she answered as she reached across and gave Carl a pat on the arm. "My daddy always said, 'You can always look around and see someone worse off than you are.' I do believe he's right."

Shaking his head in agreement he answered, "Guess he's right about that."

Further discussion on the way home included their plans for the spring garden, the corn crop and their hopes for the future. They both agreed, they had made the right decision when they moved to Colorado.

Georgene Pearson

7

Holidays

Thanksgiving was a beautiful day spent with Grandpa and Grandma Miller. Uncle Ollie, Uncle Lou and Uncle Claude, and their families, all came from Kansas for the holiday. It had been a long time since the families had all been able to be together. The children enjoyed playing and the adults had lots of visiting to catch up on. They all enjoyed the good food.

Winter hit full blast shortly after Thanksgiving. Temperatures were several degrees below freezing and the blowing winds made it even colder. It seemed like there was nothing between the prairie and the north pole to stop the winds.

They had plenty of fuel as the crop was good. Carl would shell the corn and store the cattle, and they'd burn the corncobs in the cookstove as well as the heater. Every morning they'd start a fire as it would go out at night. During the day Geneva kept the children's bedroom door closed, and also the door was closed into the storage room. The other two rooms were kept quite warm and comfortable during the day. The colder weather did bring warm memories and anticipation of the coming Christmas.

Monday after the Thanksgiving Holidays the children were in school again. After the morning exercises Miss Emory announced, "Boys and girls, I have decided on the Christmas play for this year. We will discuss the play after last recess period until time to go home. There will be parts for everyone."

You could hear some 'oohs' like 'oh goodie' and then you could hear some 'aahs' like 'oh no!' Miss Emory just ignored their reactions for right now as she knew they would like the play. It was a very cold day so they would be inside. They just might be able to discuss it some at noon.

Mary Louise was excited. She always liked to be in the Christmas play. The morning went rather quickly and some of the students gathered around to read some of the play during the noon lunch break.

"We will do our regular cleanup before we start discussing the play," Miss Emory announced after ringing the bell to get the students' attention.

Quickly the little classroom was in order and Miss Emory began, "I have selected *A Prairie Family's Christmas* for our play."

The title caught Mary Louise's attention right away as this was her family's first Christmas on the prairie. Of course, for most of the children who had always lived on the prairie it didn't seem to be anything special.

Miss Emory continued, "This story will begin at the home of the James family on Christmas Eve. The setting will be mother, daddy and three children gathered around a Christmas tree in their living room. Daddy will be pretending to read the Christmas story from the Bible. We will have a narrator or storyteller who will be reading the script. While the Christmas story is being read, other children will be pantomiming the actions. No one will have to memorize any speaking parts you will be just acting out the story."

Hands began going up when Miss Emory paused. She took time to answer their questions. She did go on to say, "We'll need good readers for the story tellers so everyone will be able to hear."

First she asked for volunteers for the narrator. Several hands went up. Miss Emory selected Brenda Baker and Mel Huff as the girl and boy storytellers. Then she listed all the characters on the chalkboard – mother, daddy, two sons, one daughter, Mary, Joseph, innkeeper, shepherds, angels and three wise men.

There were eighteen students, eleven boys and seven girls. They would need girls for the mother, daughter, Mary and narrator; that would leave three girls to be angels. The boys would be a narrator, daddy, two sons, Joseph, the innkeeper, three wise men and two shepherds. It didn't take long to get the cast chosen. Everyone seemed to be happy about the part they were going to be. Since Mary Louise's name was Mary, Miss Emory said she could be the Mother of Jesus in the play.

The teacher went on to explain that they would have to have a decorated Christmas tree. Everyone could help decorate it. They'd string cranberries and popcorn and make some paper decorations. It would be the main prop in the family's living room, along with some small chairs for the children and a couple of rocking chairs for mother and daddy.

There was a small manger at the school but they would need some straw and a doll for the manger scene. Miss Emory told the children they would just use blankets and towels for costumes for Joseph, the innkeeper, shepherds and wise men. The angels could use sheets. She wanted to keep it simple.

Mr. Fry's students would be singing the Christmas carols for the play. The play would be Sunday afternoon, December twenty-first at two-thirty in the afternoon.

When four o'clock came the children were really excited. The school bus was buzzing with the excitement of the Christmas play. Some of the children had saved part of their lunch. They were talking and eating a sandwich or cookie at the same time.

The children's voices bubbled with excitement while making plans for the play. Carl overheard the children pick Mary Louise to be the Mother of Jesus.

As Mary Louise got off the bus she pleaded, "Daddy don't tell Mama about the play. I'll change my clothes and watch Louis until you come back."

"Okay Dear, it's your secret this time," answered her daddy as he headed to the barn to help finish up the chores. Geneva always had chores started now that the days were shorter and it got dark earlier.

chapter

Christmas Play

The Pleasant Hill Schools had plenty of excitement and were very busy the next few weeks. The children were helping with ideas for props for the play, discussing their costumes, and decorating the Christmas tree and the school. The older students were practicing the Christmas carols.

Friday the nineteenth was to be the dress rehearsal. Everyone had their blankets, towels and sheets ready so they could go through the whole play from start to finish. Mr. Fry was bringing his students to sing the carols, too.

The Christmas tree was beautifully decorated and stood in the front left corner of the room. ___ was laid on the floor for a rug. Three sm___ ___ children and two rocking chairs for m___ ___ set around the tree.

The manger sce___ ___ up in the middle of the room where Miss Emory's desk usually sat. A star was hung from the ceiling above the straw filled manger.

The scene with the shepherds and angels was on the right side of the room. A large star hung above where they would kneel. The carolers would be standing along each wall so they could be seen and heard.

The dress rehearsal took all morning and then they all had a break for lunch. They did get to bundle up and go outside to play some games during the noon recess. Today was the last day of school so Miss Emory had told the children they would play games and have their Christmas party in the afternoon.

The children had drawn names to exchange gifts. No one was to spend money; they were just making little gifts for each other.

41

The afternoon passed quickly with games, refreshments and opening presents. Miss Emory had a handmade bookmark for each child.

As Miss Emory was getting the children and their things together to leave she reminded them, "Be sure and be here Sunday at one-thirty. Remember to go to Mr. Fry's room. We will all get ready there."

The students were really excited. As they were leaving the building and headed for the buses they were chanting, "School's out! School's out! The teachers let the bulls out!"

The weekend passed quickly. It was soon Sunday, the day of the school Christmas Program. Carl and Geneva had the morning farm chores done and dinner finished in plenty of time to get to the schoolhouse. Mary Louise and Louis stayed at the house. It was really too cold for them to be outside. Geneva laid out the clothes the children were going to wear.

"Come on Louis, we've got to get dressed," encouraged Mary Louise, "We're going to the play."

"Play, we gona ta play!" he laughed.

Mary Louise knew he didn't understand so she just said, "You are going to watch sister's play."

He didn't seem to object to getting dressed for he knew they were going somewhere to play.

By the time they got to the schoolhouse, quite a few people were already there. The children gathered in Mr. Fry's room as they were told and the parents were gathering in Miss Emory's room. There were no curtains nor stage but you could tell the play would be in the front of the room. The little classroom was pretty crowded by the time the students started to file across the playground.

The choir students came first led by Mr. Fry and took their places along each side of the room. They were well scrubbed with shiny faces and dressed in their best. The two storytellers followed and took their places near the little living room. The choir began to sing *Silent Night* and the rest of the cast found their places.

Next came the James family: mother, daddy, two sons and a daughter. They took their places standing around the Christmas tree. The next group to enter was the two shepherds. They walked up the aisle looking around and grinning at the crowd then knelt below the star on the right side of the room. The angels followed and knelt behind them. The innkeeper walked to the front and stood near the manger. Mary, Joseph and the three wise men waited with Miss Emory and Mr. Fry at the back of the room.

When everyone was in their place, Miss Emory signaled the storytellers to begin.

Brenda began to read, "Come sit down, children. I am going to read you the Christmas story from the Bible before you go to bed."

Mother picked up the Bible and handed it to daddy and they all sat down nicely in their chairs. Brenda continued, "I'm going to read the Christmas story from Luke chapter two." Daddy pretended he was reading the Bible.

As Mel began to read, Mary and Joseph walked slowly down the aisle and stood in front of the innkeeper.

"And it came to pass in those days, that there went out a decree from Caesar Augustus, that all the world should be taxed. And this taxing was first made when Cyrenius was governor of Syria. And all went to be taxed, everyone into his own city. And Joseph also went up from Galilee, out of the city of Nazareth, into Judea, unto the city of David, which is called Bethlehem; because he was of the house and lineage of David: To be taxed with Mary his espoused wife, being great with child."

Brenda continued the reading as the innkeeper motioned 'no room' but pointed to the manger.

"And so it was, that, while they were there, the days were accomplished that she should be delivered. And she brought forth her firstborn son, and wrapped him in swaddling clothes, and laid him in a manger; because there was no room for them in the inn."

As the choir sang, *Away in a Manger* the innkeeper walked away, Mary and Joseph lay the baby in the manger. Mary did have some problem getting the baby in the manger just like she wanted. She moved him several times.

After the choir finished, Mel began to read as one angel stood with outstretched arms.

"And there were in the same country shepherds abiding in the field, keeping watch over their flock by night. And, lo, the angel of the Lord came upon them, and the glory of the Lord shone round about them: and they were sore afraid."

As the shepherds stood the choir sang *While Shepherds Watch Their Flocks*. Brenda read. "And the angel said unto them, 'Fear not for, behold, I bring you good tidings of great joy, which shall be to all people, For unto you is born this day in the city of David, a Savior, which is Christ the Lord'."

As Mel began to read the other angels stood with open arms. By now the first angel was getting wiggly and restless.

"And this shall be a sign unto you; Ye shall find the babe wrapped in swaddling clothes, lying in a manger, and suddenly there was with the angel a multitude of heavenly hosts praising God, and saying, 'Glory to God in the highest, and on earth peace, good will toward men'."

As the angels and shepherds sat the choir sang *Hark the Herald Angels Sing*. Then Brenda read while the shepherds rose and slowly walked to the manger.

"And it came to pass, as the angels were gone away from them into heaven, the shepherds said one to another, 'Let us now go even unto Bethlehem, and see this thing which is come to pass, which the Lord hath made known unto us'. And they came with haste, and found Mary, and Joseph, and the babe lying in a manger."

One little shepherd stepped on his blanket and sort of stumbled to the manger. The children around the Christmas tree were getting restless and looking around. They snickered when the shepherd stumbled.

Then Brenda began to read, "Now children we will read about the wise men coming in Matthew chapter two." Daddy turned the pages in the Bible.

As Mel read, the three wise men walked down the aisle carrying their gifts.

"When they heard the king, they departed; and, lo, the star, which they saw in the east, went before them, till it came and stood over where the young child was. And when they were come into the house, they saw the young child with Mary his mother, and fell down and worshipped him; and when they had opened their treasures, they presented unto him gifts: gold, frankincense, and myrrh."

The choir sang, *We Three Kings*. Brenda concluded by reading, "That is the end of the Christmas story children, it is now time for you to go to bed." The children kissed their parents goodnight. Then all the children said in unison, "Goodnight," and all joined in with the choir to sing, *We Wish You A Merry Christmas*.

The audience clapped, they stood up and continued to clap. All the students went to the front and took a bow.

Mr. Fry and Miss Emory walked to the front and also took a bow. Mr. Fry waited for everyone to be seated then said, "We want to thank you for coming today. I want to thank Miss Emory and all the students for the hard work that's gone into getting ready for this play. Thanks to the choir for all the fine singing of the Christmas carols. The school board has a Christmas sack for all the children as you leave. Thanks again for coming, Merry Christmas and A Happy New Year!"

The little schoolhouse was like a beehive while friends, families, and neighbors visited and congratulated all the little performers. Students made it to the back real fast to get their sacks. It wasn't long before everyone had left for home and the doors were locked until after New Year's Day.

The Millers were home shortly as they lived just one-and-a-half miles east of the school, but Daddy and Mama both had time to tell Mary Louise how nice the play was and that she made a beautiful mother for Baby Jesus.

chapter

Prairie Christmas

Now that school was out for the holiday, time could be spent finishing up plans for Christmas at home.

"Your daddy has gone to find a small dead tree over along the creek," Mother was telling Mary Louise as they were finishing breakfast dishes. "We're going to decorate it like we did when I was a little girl."

"But there aren't any evergreen trees on the creek, Mama."

"I know, dear, that's why we're going to decorate a little tree like I use to. We just can't buy an evergreen tree this year."

"Just how did you decorate your tree when you were little?" she asked as she just couldn't ~~~~~~~ her mind.

"Well, my daddy ~~~~~~~~~~~ small dead tree and then my mama would ~~~~~~~~ rags and we'd wrap all the branches. Then we'd ~~~~ paper decorations, paper chains and popcorn chains and hang them on it. We'd put real candles on the branches."

"That sounds like fun!" she exclaimed. "Miss Emory let me have come chains and decorations from the tree at school. We can use them too. But, what will we do for candles?" she inquired as she hadn't seen any candles at their house.

Mama turned to her daughter, smiled and said, "Your daddy and I planned this several weeks ago. When we took the cream to Holly one week we stopped at Bean's Drug Store and picked out some candles and some colored paper."

"Oh! Mama, did you? When can I start making decorations?" she asked as she was hanging up the dish towel.

47

"Since it's really too cold for you to be outside, you can get started right away. If Daddy can find a tree today, we can work on it tonight after supper.

Mama got out the small red candles; the red, white and green paper; and the scissors. Mary Louise brought out the decorations and chains that Miss Emory had given to her. She also brought her crayons and pencil. She was ready to begin.

"Mama the candles are beautiful but how do they stay on the tree?"

"I'll just have to show you when we get the tree ready."

While Carl and Geneva finished the chores Mary Louise was busy making white angels and red and green Christmas balls which she decorated with her crayons. She cut out snowflakes too. She had learned how to fold and cut paper to make really fancy snowflakes.

"I wanta color too," begged Louis as he watched his sister. So she cut out some paper circles for him to color.

By evening the children had lots of decorations made and were anxious to get the tree decorated. Daddy had found a small tree about five feet tall and sort of skinny. He had put it in a bucket of sod so it would stand up straight.

The house smelled like popcorn as Mama had popped several skillets of popcorn and put it in a deep pan. They all nibbled on the popcorn as they worked on the tree.

She brought out an old thin and patched sheet. "I'll tear this into narrow strips. Then you can wrap each branch so it is completely covered," Mama said as she took a narrow strip of material and began to wrap it around and around.

"This is really fun! It will make our tree look like it's covered with snow, won't it, Daddy?"

Mama handed Daddy a strip of cloth and he began to wrap a branch and said, "This is all right, Dear."

The whole family laughed, talked and wrapped until the little brown tree was completely covered. It did look like it was covered with snow now.

Mama got her needle and thread. She put a string in all the carefully made ornaments so they would hang.

Soon there were lots of bright paper decorations hanging on the tree. Daddy put a beautiful little angel on the very top. He had to hang the decorations that were too high for the children to reach. They let Louis hang the ones around the bottom.

After all the decorations were on, Daddy snapped the metal candleholders on the end of the branches.

"So that's the way you do it!" Mary Louise exclaimed as she was carefully watching. She got to put the little red candles in each holder, except the ones that were too high on the tree.

"Now we need to make some popcorn chains," Mama said as she began to put a long thread in her needle. She fixed a needle for Mary Louise and Daddy too.

"Louis you can hand us the popcorn," Mama was saying as she moved the pan of popcorn over to a chair. They all sat down and started threading kernels of popcorn on their strings.

Mama tied all the strings together. Daddy and Mary Louise draped them around the tree.

"Now our Christmas tree smells like popcorn," laughed Mary Louise as she hung the last string. "It even makes it seem like there is fluffy white snow covering our tree."

Daddy moved it back a little into the corner. They just stood there and admired the unusual little tree. "It did turn out beautiful, didn't it?" Mary Louise was saying as she turned and gave her folks a delightful smile.

"Of course, Dear." Mama was pleased that she liked it. "It's like the tree I had when I was a little girl. I always thought they were beautiful too," answered her mama as she was remembering Christmas in Oklahoma many years ago.

"When can we light the candles?" she asked as she reached out and carefully touched one.

"Let's light them now, Mama," Carl said looking across at Geneva. "I'm kinda anxious to see the candles burning myself."

"ight! ight! andles!" was the excited echo heard across the room.

"Go ahead, Carl, get the matches, we all want to see what the tree looks like with the candles lit."

Daddy got the matches. He lit the candles around the top and then down the sides and around the bottom. Mama blew out the kerosene lamp. They watched the lights twinkle on the branches.

"It is so beautiful!" Mary Louise said in a gasp as she stood looking at the fluffy snowwhite tree now sparkling from the yellow flickering lights.

"Guess we'd better blow them out for now," advised Mama. "We'll light them again Christmas Eve for awhile and then Christmas morning when we open presents.

"Will Santa find us this year? Will he know that we have moved to Colorado?" asked Mary Louise hopefully.

"Santa always knows where you are, so don't you worry," assured her daddy as he smiled at Geneva.

Christmas morning Mama slipped into the children's bedroom, "Wake up! you sleepy heads, it's Christmas!" she was saying as she pulled back the covers.

That's all it took to get them out of bed and out to the Christmas tree in their pj's.

"Just look, Louis, Santa did find us. He did know that we had moved!" she was exclaiming to her little brother as they knelt in front of the little old fashioned tree.

Daddy had lit the candles and they seemed to be twinkling even brighter this morning. Guess that was because of the shadows that were dancing on the walls behind the tree and maybe some sleep still in their eyes.

Beneath the branches were several packages of different sizes and shapes brightly wrapped and tied with colorful bows.

"Guess we'd better find out what's in those packages," Daddy said with a grin and handed each one a box to unwrap.

It didn't take long until they had the packages torn open. There was a red truck for Louis and a small teddy bear. Also some new yellow pj's with little animals on them and some yellow yarn slippers. Another box had a new blue shirt. "Ooh! ook!" was all he could say.

Mary Louise's first package had a pair of blue polka dot pj's and blue yarn slippers. She also had a rag doll with red yarn hair. The biggest box had a new red plaid dress. The last package was a book, *Alice In Wonderland*. "Oh, just what I wanted!" she exclaimed.

Mary Louise was so excited she forgot about the special present she had for Mama and Daddy. She slipped off to her bedroom and got the package. It was rolled up with a red piece of yarn tied around it.

"Here, Mama, Daddy – surprise!" she said so excited she could hardly wait for them to open it. "I made it at school."

Mama untied the yarn and unrolled the paper.

"Why, Honey! What a surprise!" Mama said as she was showing it to Carl. "This is you – it's a silhouette picture of you! Isn't it nice, Carl?"

While Mama and Daddy continued to look at the picture Mary Louise was saying, "Miss Emory helped us make our pictures. She let us sit by the kerosene lamp and she traced around our shadow. We got to cut them out of black paper and paste them on the white paper."

"It is so nice, Dear, and thank you so much," Mama was saying and giving her little girl a big hug.

Daddy smiled as he handed a surprise package to Mama. She opened it. There was pink and blue striped material to make a dress.

"Why, Carl, that's the gingham material that I saw at the JC Penney Company for ten cents a yard!"

Daddy looked over at Mary Louise and winked but Mama caught him.

"Oh, so you told Daddy what material I liked, didn't you?" Mama said jokingly. "I sure am glad you were with me that day we shopped at JC Penney. You sure have a good memory, too."

Geneva had made Carl a blue and red shirt from some feed sacks she had been saving. "Now, when did you ever have time to make a shirt for me?" Carl asked looking around at all the things she had made for the children. "I just don't know how you did it all." He was so proud of her.

"You know we'd better blow out those candles before we burn the house down," Mama was saying as she started blowing out the candles. She was soon joined by the rest of the family blowing just as hard as they could.

chapter

10

School Project

The happy time spent at home with family during Christmas passed too quickly for Mary Louise. There had been special goodies to eat, new gifts to share and enjoy, and even plenty of fun playing in the new-fallen snow.

The little Christmas tree with all of it's colorful decorations was just a pleasant memory.

January 1931 was the beginning of a new year. Looking back, the prairie family was grateful for all the good things of the past. The future seemed to hold only the best. Dreams were coming to pass in spite of the struggles and changes of the past few months.

School began again on Monday, the fourth. Snow covered the ground but the group was happy to be together again. It was cold on the way to school but twenty warm bodies and noisy laughter made them forget about the cold.

Miss Emory welcomed everyone back to school. She gave them time to tell about their Christmas and vacation time. Of course, Mary Louise had taken her new book, *Alice In Wonderland*, to show. She was hoping Miss Emory would want to read it aloud.

Miss Emory asked, "Would you like to share your book with the whole class? I'd love to read it aloud."

"I sure would," she answered. She had read it during Christmas vacation but it was soooooo good. She knew Miss Emory would really make it come to life. She liked to listen to her read aloud. She'd change her voice for the different characters. She liked to watch her face and hands as she dramatized every scene.

After lunch Miss Emory announced, "Boys and girls, we're going to begin work on a unit in social studies. I believe you will

53

all enjoy it. We're going to be working together." She had the attention of everyone.

"What were they going to do that all the grades could do together?" thought Mary Louise.

Miss Emory continued, "We're going to begin a study about people of other lands. Well let the older students help the younger ones find stories and help them read. After you've read about a group of people, you'll write down what you find. We'll put this information together to make a book."

Mary Louise looked around the room. She could see that some of the children had eager looks on their faces; others looked blank and confused. She wasn't really sure that she understood but since they were going to do it together, she knew it would be all right. Miss Emory always helped you when you needed it.

"Do you have any questions?" she was asking. Right away hands began to go up from some of the older students.

"What people will we study first?" asked Mabel.

"I'll put a list on the chalkboard. Well do a study about each one. Then you may choose which people you want to put in your book. I'll tell you how many different people each grade will have to have."

"Where will we find this information about these different people?" inquired Mel.

"I have chosen books from our library shelf about different groups. We also have our set of encyclopedias that you may use. Some of you may have some books at home that you'd like to share."

Another student asked, "How will we work together? Will we work in groups?"

Miss Emory explained, "Yes, we will work in groups. When we decide which people we will study first, we will all try to find out something about those people."

She turned to the chalkboard and wrote a list of things to look for – country, home, clothes, food and climate.

"This is some of the information you might be looking for about each group of people. You might even think of some-thing more too."

Mary Louise raised her hand.

"Yes, Mary Louise," said Miss Emory.

"We might want to know about their families."

"You are right. We can add that to our list," answered Miss Emory as she turned to add families to the list on the chalkboard.

Some of the other children had questions so the discussion continued until Miss Emory was sure everyone understood.

"Now we must decide which people we want to study. Who has a suggestion?" she asked. In no time there was a list of people of other lands – Eskimos, Dutch, Indians, Japanese, Spanish and Africans.

The children decided they would begin with the Eskimo people first. So, Miss Emory divided the children into four groups. They spent the rest of the day reading, sharing books, and writing down what they could find about the Eskimos.

Finally, Miss Emory rang the bell on her desk, which meant it was time to put everything away and get ready to go home.

"Be sure to keep all your papers together so we can share and discuss the information tomorrow," she told the children.

Already excitement was growing as the students were reading and comparing information. It seemed like this project would keep the children busy. They'd be having to spend a lot of time indoors for the next several weeks as the weather was too cold to be outdoors.

For the next six weeks of school, the children spent a part of the day working on the social studies project. It took about a week on each group of people – reading, discussing, writing, correcting and rewriting their reports. Last of all, they made the covers and put the books together. Miss Emory was very pleased with the work of the students.

Mary Louise had been telling her parents about the book they were making in social studies. She was interested in other people of the world.

When the project was finished she was very proud to bring her book home. She told her daddy about it on the bus as they were going home.

"We'll look at your book when we get home. Mama will want to see it too," he said as he gave her his approving smile.

"I hope Mama hasn't gone to the barn yet. I can hardly wait to show it to her."

As soon as Daddy stopped the bus, she dashed off to the house. "Oh Mama," she called from the back door, "are you here, Mama?"

"Yes, I'm here. What's wrong?" she asked.

"Nothing is wrong, I was just hoping you hadn't left for the barn yet. I got to bring home my social studies book and I want you to read it!" she was saying almost out of breath by now.

She quickly unpacked her school things to find the treasured little book and handed it proudly to her Mama. Carl came in just as Geneva sat down and started to look at the book.

"Daddy, come look at my book that I've been telling you about!"

So, Carl and Geneva sat down at the table and opened the book as Mary Louise stood proudly beside her Daddy.

"See. I wanta see," her little brother said as he pulled on Mama's dress.

Geneva picked him up and sat him on her lap. They closed the book and started over, showing him the cover. It was a half of a sheet of brown construction paper. A black circle was pasted in the center. A smaller white circle with a black silhouette person was pasted on the black circle. Across the bottom was neatly printed, *People of Other Lands*. Two brads held the little book together. Mama turned the page and read

"The Eskimo toy are made of bone.
The Eskimo toy are woodpecker and a toy
bear and two toy dogs.
The Eskimo lives in a snow house.
The Eskimo eat meat for their dinner.
It is cold where the Eskimo lives.
The Eskimo are happy."

They turned the page. The next people in the book were Indians. She read

"1. The Indian is red.
2. The Indian lives in tents.
3. The Indian eats birds.
4. The Indian boys wear moccasins.
5. They make their houses of hides and skins.
6. The Indian wear skin clothes.
7. The Indian eat fish.
8. Their shoes are made of skin."
Mama turned the page.

"Let me read this page," Mary Louise said and she began to read

"1. In Japan there are Islands.
2. The Japan children wear wooden shoes.
3. In summer it is hot.
4. The Japan children mother carries them on her back.
   All live in a hut."

The next page was a blank sheet of lined paper. The brown construction paper made the back of her book.

"That's all," she said and Mama closed the book.

"That is so nice and you learned all of that at school, didn't you?" Geneva asked as she looked at the little book again. "We will want to save this so we can read it again."

"That's quite a book. You can read it to Louis again while Mama and I get the chores done. After supper you can read it again to Mama and me," said her daddy proudly.

11

Valentines

The prairie winter days were much shorter now. The cold biting winds had made the farm chores much more difficult. It took more time to feed and care for the animals. Carl had to break the ice in the cattle tank at the windmill so the cows could have water to drink.

They always had to make sure there were several tubs of corncobs in the storage room for fuel. Geneva dreaded wash days. It was so cold to carry water from the windmill. It took more corncobs to heat the water.

She had two wash tubs – one to wash and scrub the clothes using a washboard and homema~~de~~ . She'd use the other tub to rinse the clot~~he~~ water out by hand. The hardest part wa~~s~~ line in the freezing winds. The clothes w~~ere~~ stiff as she hung them up. Their overalls, shirts and dresses looked like headless frozen people fighting back at the crisp blowing winds.

Ironing wasn't such a chore as it was always warm by the kitchen stove where she heated the flat irons. As she ironed today she had plenty of time to think. She even told Louis the story of the *Three Little Pigs* and sang some nursery songs. It made the time pass much more quickly.

"A few more weeks of winter then spring will be welcomed with open arms," she thought. "There will be so much to do when warmer weather is here to stay."

A glance at the clock let her know that it was almost four-thirty. Carl and Mary Louise would be coming home soon. She stopped ironing to get their afternoon snack ready.

When the door opened a wave of cold air swept across the little kitchen. A bouncing little girl came in with rosy red cheeks from the stinging cold.

"Hello, Mama!" she said as she took off her wraps and overshoes. "Guess what? We're going to have a Valentine Party at school!"

"Oh, you are! When will that be?" her mama asked.

"On Friday the thirteenth as Valentine's Day is really on Saturday."

Carl hung his coat and hat in the storage room. He left his overshoes there too, then came on into the kitchen. He listened as Mary Louise told them all about school and the Valentine Party.

Mama had set out the milk and cookies. This was their special time together and everyone enjoyed sitting around the table.

"We're going to decorate a big box and all the valentines will go into it. Miss Emory is going to read us a story about St. Valentines. She said we remember him like we do the Presidents of the United States."

"That will be interesting, won't it?" answered Mama.

"I guess I've forgotten why we remember St. Valentine myself," Carl said.

Mama replied, "I don't remember either. You'll have to find out and tell us all about it."

"May Louis and I make some valentines here, Mama?" she asked. "We do have some red and white paper left from Christmas don't we?"

"I forgot all about that paper. We sure do. That would be very nice," Mama said thoughtfully. "You could make some for your brother to color too."

Mama put away the glasses and cookie plate. Then she got the leftover red and white paper. She also got the scissors. Mary Louise brought out her crayons and a pencil.

"We're going to make some valentines," she told her little brother, who was always right on her heels when she came home from school.

"Tine, make tines!" he was saying as he followed her to the kitchen table.

"Here is an old catalog. You can use some of the pages to make different size heart patterns," Mama explained. "Do you remember how to fold the paper so you can make a nice heart pattern?"

"Miss Emory showed us today at school. I already remembered from last year. Miss Andrews showed us how to do it."

"Now that you two have something to do here by the fire, it's time for Mama and me to get the chores done before it gets too dark," Daddy said as he pushed his chair back.

As Daddy added a few more corncobs to the fire he said, "Mr. Romer said he'd heard we might have an early spring – sounds good to me," he continued.

"I was thinking about that today myself," answered Geneva. "It sure can't come too early for me. Maybe February will be our last cold month."

The children kept busy cutting, coloring and pasting. They had some nice valentines by the time the evening chores were finished.

"These are practice valentines," she told her mama and daddy and she showed them their valentines. "Now I'll know what to make at school."

Miss Emory brought a big box to school the next day. She had some red and white paper to cover it. After the children finished their work in the afternoon, they worked on decorating the box. They made heart people and pasted them on it, also heart animals and heart plants. It was a colorful valentine box all right. Then they started making valentines for each other.

There were plenty of valentines in the box the day of the party. It was a beautiful day. The sun was shining brightly. A gentle breeze was blowing from the south. The last snow was gone except in the shady areas. The children were able to bundle up and even play some running games outside at recess. They really liked to choose up sides and play Fox and Geese.

At lunch time Miss Emory said, "We will not have classes after the afternoon recess."

Everyone laughed and clapped for joy. They were thrilled about the Valentine Party.

"It will take quite awhile to pass out all the valentines," she continued when the clapping stopped.

When they came in from the last recess Miss Emory moved the valentine box to the front of the room. "Boys and girls, you will all have a turn to pass out the cards. We'll start with the first graders, then move on up with each grade." Everyone clapped again.

She opened the lid and each of the first graders reached in and got a few valentines. Miss Emory helped them read the names, then they proudly delivered each card they had.

As the children continued to pass out valentines, some of them were opening theirs and reading the little verses that had been carefully written. There seemed to be a lot of verses that read

"Roses are red,
Violets are blue,
Sugar is sweet
And so are you!"

Miss Emory had homemade heart-shape cookies for everyone. This was her valentine surprise.

"Time passes so quickly when you are having fun," thought Mary Louise, and today they were having fun with all the pictures and verses on their valentines.

It was soon time to gather up their treasures and get ready to go home. Mary Louise could hardly wait to show her family all the valentines she had. She'd have to read them every little verse. Her favorite was

"Valentine, I'd walk a mile For your Smile!"

Carl had some valentines too. Some of the children had made cards for him with neat little pictures and cute rhyming verses.

chapter

12

Spring

March came in like a lamb, would it go out like a lion? A spacious blue canopy covered the prairie as far as one could see. The bright sun seemed to wipe away the cold, chilly memories of snow and ice. Warm southerly winds dried the ground enough that the farmers were preparing to plant their spring crops. Families were choosing seeds for planting their spring gardens. It seemed like a beautiful new beginning.

Children were enjoying being out of doors again. Mary Louise was all excited one evening when she came home from school. "Guess what, Mama?" she asked. "We got to go barefoot at school today."

"It's getting warmer. The first day of spring was almost a week ago. _____ the corner."

"When is Easter, _____ asked.

"We'll have to check the calendar," Mama answered.

As Carl came in Mama and Mary Louise were looking at the calendar. "Looks like my ladies are making plans – are you going to clue me in?" he jokingly asked.

"We were just talking about spring being here and just checking to see when Easter is," Geneva answered.

"Well, when is Easter?" asked Carl.

Mama said, "Today is Wednesday the twenty-fifth, and April first is a week from today." She turned the page and stated, "Easter is April fifth this year."

"That's less than two weeks away," remarked Carl, "My goodness time is flying. I'm going to have to get that corn field worked again as it will soon be time to plant."

63

Mary Louise could hardly wait for her daddy to finish talking as she wanted to tell him about the Easter Egg hunt they were going to have at school. Miss Emory had already told the children about the egg hunt. She had said they'd make more plans the next week.

The evening chores seemed to get finished early now that the days were longer. Louis and Mary Louise had even had time to play outside.

"May I saddle Prince and take Louis for a ride?" she asked running into the barn.

"Just ride around the buildings and don't go out into the road," warned her Daddy. "You'll have to give him some oats when you bring him back."

"Okay, Daddy," she yelled. "I can do that."

So, Carl and Geneva finished the evening chores. Mary Louise and Louis rode Prince around the farmyard.

"Orsie, wide!" Louis giggled. He liked riding Prince too.

"Hold on tight to the saddle horn," she told him and showed him the saddle horn, then she took the reins.

"Old on!" he repeated after her.

Finally Carl said, "Guess it's time to put Prince up. Mama has supper ready and it'll soon be dark." He took Louis off the pony and watched as Mary Louise started trotting Prince back to the barn.

"Take him to get a drink first," her Daddy called.

Mary Louise always took good care of Prince. She took him to the horse tank then on to the barn to feed him his oats and hay.

"Thanks for the ride ole pal," she said as she dumped the oats in the manger. "I'll see ya later and we'll go for a long ride," she assured him with a pat.

The next day began as usual. Carl left about seven-thirty on the bus route. He'd be back by to pick up Mary Louise about eight twenty. When Mary Louise was dressed and ready for school Geneva said, "I'm going to go on to the barn and start the milking. Be sure you listen for Daddy to honk the horn so he won't have to wait on you. Don't forget to take your coat."

"Oh, I won't forget, Mama," she answered.

"Louis, you stay in the house and wait for Daddy. He'll be back in a little while and bring you down to the barn."

The prairie sky was open and magnificent. She knew Louis would enjoy being outside. Geneva dressed in her barn clothes and headed to the barn. "It sure is warm this morning," she thought. "I won't be needing this jacket for long." She looked across the vast treeless landscape extending to the horizon. The sun was already up and spreading a warm path across the fields. "My what a beautiful day!" she said to herself.

Even the farm animals seemed to be happy about it. The chickens were out pecking for bugs in the yard and clucking. The pigs were running around in their pens and squealing. The cows were standing in the corral chewing their cud and looking contented.

Geneva looked to the western sky and could see some gray clouds on the horizon. "We just might get a spring rain before the day is over," she thought.

She put the feed in the manger and turned in the cows. She got her three-legged stool and milk pail. As she sat down to milk, the warm sunshine filtered through the cracks on the east side of the barn making the barn dust dance across her feet. The quick squeeze of her fingers right-left right-left, made a ping ping musical sound as the streams of warm milk hit the bottom of the pail.

Her pleasure-filled thoughts were interrupted by the honking of the bus horn. She paused and looked through the sunshine slanting through the cracks. Mary Louise came flying out the door and raced down the driveway. Her little unbuttoned coat was flapping in the south breeze. "She's quite the girl and so full of life." Geneva continued to think about how proud she was of her and how she'd grown since they'd been out here on the farm.

Later the cows started acting up and some of them got out in the corral. She went out to get them back in and was surprised to see it was snowing beautiful fluffy flakes with the sun still shining!

"Those clouds had looked like rain," she said aloud to herself. "It's awfully late to be having snow and it's so warm."

The south winds made the snowflakes bounce around so beautifully. "This won't last long," she thought as she got the cows back into the barn.

Later she noticed it was getting colder and the sun was covered with clouds. She looked out the barn door. The wind was out of the north now and blowing harder. She decided to hang up the milk pails and go to the house to check on Louis. She sure didn't want him out in this. Carl would be back before long and they could go back and finish the chores then.

As she headed to the house, which was only about 250 feet from the barn, the snow was already so thick she could hardly hold her eyes open. The wind seemed to be getting stronger too. She hung up her clothes. She'd have to wait for Carl to come back now.

13

Snowday

Carl went out to the bus around seven-thirty to start his route as usual. It was such a beautiful morning. A warm gentle breeze was sweeping across the prairie. "He didn't need a coat after all," he thought, "but he wouldn't take it back to the house now."

As he turned east from his driveway, the sun was already shining in his eyes. He reached up and pulled down the sun visor to shade his eyes. "This will be a good day to get the garden ground plowed," he thought.

Some of the children were chatty, as usual, others were still and quiet like they were hardly awake. When he turned back and headed west he could see some dark looking clouds hanging in the sky. "Looks like we might get some rain sometime today," he said to the children as he stopped to pick up Mary Louise. "We could use some rain, too."

He turned north to pick up the Teague's four children and Crissie Smithover as she was working there now. "Those clouds are moving in fast," he said to Ryan, the last one to get on the bus.

Shortly he thought he was running into some fog but instead they were fluffy snowflakes with the sun shining behind them. The last mile south to the schoolhouse the children were really excited. There were large fluffy snowflakes floating in the gentle breeze. The children could hardly believe their eyes nor wait to get to school so they could play in the snow.

By the time they arrived at the schoolhouse the playground was covered with snow. The children started to gather up their books and lunches when Carl said, "Just leave your things on the bus, we just may be going home."

The children really whooped it up then. "Yea! Snow! No school!" They jumped out and headed for the playground.

"This is unbelievable!" Claude and Ryan yelled.

"Snow, let's have a snowball fight." That's all it took for the snowballs to start flying.

Some of the children gathered between the two schoolhouses to start a game of Fox and Geese in the snow. One child was the fox and as the geese ran from one side to the other, he would try to catch them. If you were caught then you had to help the fox catch the others. They were chasing each other and having a barrel of fun.

Carl had gone inside to talk to Miss Emory, and Mr. Fry was there. They were standing by the window looking out at the swirling snow and dark clouds.

"You know," Carl said as he stepped inside, "it is really snowing out there! I could hardly see down the road by the time I got here."

"We were just looking at the clouds and discussing how fast that storm blew in here," Mr. Fry said. "The sun was shining when I came in this morning."

"I'm wondering if we should try to have school today?" Miss Emory asked. "This might be quite a storm if it lasted all day like this."

Mr. Fry replied, "Oh, I don't think this will amount to anything, it's just an early spring flurry and will probably blow over as fast as it blew in."

"Snowstorms can be dangerous out here on the prairie I've been told. It sure doesn't seem to be letting up. Is the west bus in yet?" asked Carl.

"No, he's not here yet," stated Mr. Fry.

"I'd sure feel better if the children were at home," Miss Emory's voice was showing concern. "It's hard to keep these buildings warm when it gets cold."

About that time the school door swung open and in rushed the cold noisy children. A gust of cold wind swept across the room. The children were all talking at once. "The wind has changed to the north and it's really cold out there."

"Please take your seats, children," Miss Emory said. The children sat down and the teachers continued to discuss the weather conditions. Mr. Fry went to the door and looked out. Another strong gust of wind burst into the room. "Sure enough, the wind has changed," he said. "I think you'd better put these children back on the bus and take them home. If the other bus comes, we can send them home too."

The children were quietly looking around at each other and whispering, "Goodie! Goodie! No school today!"

Carl turned from the window and said, "Mr. Fry, this storm has gotten too bad for me to be out on these prairie roads. I could barely see when I drove in awhile ago. The winds are worse now and it's getting colder."

Mr. Fry replied, "I think you can get them home before the storm gets any worse."

"It's already too difficult to see out there and the winds are getting stronger all the time. I don't think we should be out on the road," Carl said quite determined and his jaws were set. "You can hardly see the other schoolhouse now or the bus."

"You could get them home easier now before the roads get blocked," Miss Emory said. "We need to decide instead of just talking."

The teachers were trying to keep their voices down but the children knew they didn't agree. Mr. Miller was really worried about the storm since it came up so quickly. They seemed to be arguing about what to do.

Finally, Mr. Fry said, "I think you'd better get the children back on the bus and get them home as soon as possible."

Carl turned and walked reluctantly to the door. Miss Emory said to the children, "There will be no school today! Go back to the bus as quickly as you can so Mr. Miller can be on his way."

The wind was already blowing a severe gale. The older children carried the smaller ones to the bus. The children were happy to be going home. They laughed and sang as Carl cranked the engine and wiped the snow from the windshield.

He could hardly believe it had turned so cold in the last hour. As they left the schoolyard about nine o'clock and headed north-east, he couldn't see the road or the radiator cap on the front of the bus. He didn't feel good about leaving the drafty school-house for its coal stove would at least provide shelter and warmth for the children in this unpredictable arctic blast!

chapter

14

Blizzard

The storm was getting worse all the time. The temperature was dropping fast and the winds were increasing. Carl rolled the window down and tried to see the road. The wind whipped the snow in so furiously until he couldn't see anything. He was driving blindly into this raging blizzard and snowstorm.

Rose was sitting right behind Carl and he said, "Could you help me watch for the road? It's really hard to see out there."

Rose tried to help Carl watch but she couldn't see either. "Mr. Miller, I can't see anything either." She had a feeling they were going the wrong direction when they left the schoolyard.

The kids were drawing and writing their names in the steam that covered the windows wiping it off trying to see out. They were all cold it was much colder than when they got to school.

Finally, Carl decided to turn around as he just could not see. The bus engine died. He got out, raised the hood and dug out the snow. He got the engine started again. He wiped the snow piles from the windshield and got back on the bus. They continued going slowly and blindly, trying to stay on the road.

The steam on the windows was now turning to ice. Some of the children were trying to scratch it off trying to see outside. The older children were trying to watch for the road and fences.

Again the engine died. Carl got out in the blinding blizzard again to dig snow out from under the hood. After some time the children heard the engine growl to a start and they knew they'd be going again soon.

71

"Do any of you recognize anything. We ought to be coming to the Holly road or the schoolhouse," he told the children. There was nothing but a wall of whiteness. He continued to strain his eyes to find some sort of landmark and carefully continued to drive on slowly.

"We'll keep going," he said to the children. "We'll get somewhere soon."

He had stopped several times to scrape the snow from the windshield. He rolled the window down too, but it just made matters worse.

A third time the engine died. Carl was exhausted from the strain and cold but he got out and cleaned the snow from the engine and the windshield. Finally, he got the motor started. He'd try it again!

"We've been gone about forty-five minutes or an hour from the schoolhouse," he thought. "It must be about ten o'clock." He didn't want to believe they were lost but he was beginning to think so.

After traveling a short distance further he exclaimed. "Oh look! There's a fence and a road!" He started across but hit a ditch. The engine died again. At least, they'd found a road.

Carl got out and looked the situation over. He could see the back wheels were off the ground. He would not be able to get the bus out. He raised the hood and dug out the snow again. He couldn't get the engine started this time. The bus was stalled! He drained the water from the motor. "It'll run better without water than it will froze up," he thought. He knew it had to be below freezing now, maybe even below zero the way the winds were raging. He found this very hard to believe when just a couple of hours ago the sun was shining and there were only warm southerly breezes blowing across the prairie.

Carl got back on the bus wiping the freezing snow from his eyes and face. "We can't be far from a house. Someone will be along soon and get us out."

He sat down with the children on the benches. He picked up Mary Louise and sat her on his lap saying, "It'll be all right, Honey, somebody will pull us out pretty soon."

"But Daddy, I'm cold," she said.

"I know but we'll be okay." he answered trying to console her and the other children.

Ryan and Crissie asked, "Let us go look and see if we can tell where we are."

"All right," answered Carl, "but don't go far. You can hardly stand up out there."

In just a short while they were back. "We followed the ditch but we couldn't see anything through the blowing snow," they told Carl.

The younger boys, Roland, Jimmy, Lee, Joe and Jon, were bunched up together but complained about being cold, too. "Let's all huddle together," Carl suggested. "It'll help us stay warm." He knew the children were not dressed warm enough for this cold drop in temperature.

So the younger ones huddled against the older children. They began to tell jokes and laugh, trying to forget about the cold and keep their spirits up. The morning passed so slowly as they waited. What they didn't know was that the temperature had dropped to minus twenty degrees or minus thirty degrees with fierce hurricane-force winds that were blowing seventy to eighty miles per hour. That made the windchill factor near minus one hundred degrees across the prairie!

Carl thought it must be getting near noon as the children were now saying they were hungry. Carl tugged at the wooden benches until he got them up. They had to dig their lunches out of the snow. They were covered with snow and ice. The lids were frozen shut on their lunch buckets. Carl couldn't pry them open.

The howling winds had whipped the powdery snow in around the windows as if there weren't any there. It was making drifts inside the bus. There were twenty worried children and Carl being buried in this whirling freezing whiteness.

"Well, we're not going to freeze, that's a cinch," Carl said. "I'm going to build a fire! Find me a lunch bucket," he said as he got out his pocketknife and started making kindling out of the driver's seat. He took some pieces of wood out and soaked them in the gas tank. He put some of the sticks in the bottom of the can and lit them.

Smoke filled the bus. It stung their eyes and made the children cough. They took turns trying to get warm around the makeshift fire. Carl kept adding pieces of kindling until they were all gone. Then he decided to have some fun with them trying to keep their minds off the cold. "Now, you can burn your books and papers," he said as enthusiastically as he could. So the children made a game of burning history books, geography books, readers, arithmetic books, rulers and Big Chief writing tablets! The lunch bucket blazed and smoked. It provided temporary warmth for the twenty frightened and weary children as they tried to keep the smoke out of their eyes and fought to breathe in the smoke-filled bus. It was fun while it lasted. When there wasn't anything else to burn and no more matches, the fire went out. "You've got to move around," Carl said. "Wave your arms and stamp your feet."

They didn't have much space to move around in. The center aisle was only about two feet wide and eighteen feet long, so they sort of shuffled trying not to step on each other. This was very tiring for the already exhausted children.

As darkness began to fall the storm raged even more. The freight-train winds rocked the bus but it didn't rock the cold, hungry children to sleep. Carl would see to that!

chapter

15

Waiting

Geneva made it back to the house to check on Louis. Mary Louise had tied an apron around his waist. "Do dishes," he explained as Geneva untied it.

"You are a big helper too," she told him.

On the table was a stack of neatly folded clothes. "Why, Mary Louise folded these clothes while she waited on Daddy, didn't she?"

"I fol' too," Louis bragged.

"Okay little fellow, you're getting to be a big boy like sister," said Geneva picking him up and setting him on her lap. She gave him a hug and a squeeze.

"You know, I thought they would be home by now. Maybe they decided to stay at school," she told him. "I hope your daddy stayed there instead of trying to make it back home." She fixed a snack for Louis and poured a cup of leftover coffee in a cup for herself. The house was getting cold. She took Louis and went into her bedroom. The heater would keep them warm. She shut all the doors trying to keep the cold out. She had four tubs of corncobs so she'd have to use them sparingly.

They finally got in bed and covered up with blankets. It didn't take long for Louis to fall asleep. She couldn't sleep – she was worried about the school children, her husband, her daughter and the cattle.

She decided the storm was just too bad. Carl wasn't coming back this morning. After Louis was asleep she quietly got out of bed, dressed in her barn clothes, and started to the barn to finish the milking.

75

She stepped out into the raging whiteness but she couldn't see the barn or anything. She could only feel the biting snow as it stung her face. An inner voice spoke to her, "You better not go – stay with the baby."

She went back into the house, took off her barn clothes and hung them up in the storage room. She went into the bedroom to check on Louis then laid back down. The only thing she could hear was the wild howling fury of the wind.

When Louis woke up, she built a small fire in the kitchen stove and warmed the coffee again. "Would you like Mama to scramble an egg for you, honey? Are you hungry?"

"Eat – me eat," he said.

She tried to keep up small talk with the baby but she kept going to the window thinking she heard something. There was nothing but thick frost on the windowpane which seemed to be making fearful faces in the lacy ice.

They snuggled again under the heavy blankets for warmth. She even tried covering her head so she couldn't hear the noise of the howling wind as it thrashed around the house.

After some time she decided she should try to take care of the cattle. She dressed as warm as she could, determined to make it this time. As she stepped out into the howling whiteness again that same voice warned, "You'd better not go – stay with the baby."

So she undressed and hung up her clothes. Another cup of coffee would surely warm her up and calm her nerves. She hadn't eaten since breakfast, but she was too worried to eat.

Geneva watched the clock tick off the hours. Carl should be home by 4:30, if he was coming. He didn't come. "Surely they were all safe at the schoolhouse," were her convincing thoughts.

When Louis awoke she explained, "Daddy and sister probably won't be home tonight. The snow and wind are just too bad."

"Issie not come?" he asked.

"No, I'm afraid the storm just came too fast. They'll be home tomorrow."

"Morrow, Issie come," he said shaking his head.

"I need to go finish up the chores before it gets dark. Now you stay right here by the fire and don't open the doors," she warned as she put some of his toys on the bed. "Get up here," she continued, "so you can stay warm."

Again she dressed putting on the warmest clothes she could find. She was determined this wicked storm wouldn't keep her from doing the chores this time. She stepped out one more time and the hurricane winds blew icy snowflakes into her eyes until she couldn't hold them open. The voice warned her for the third time, "You better not go – stay with the baby!"

Defeated by the unpredictable storm she went back in, took off the barn clothes and hung them up. "I'll just have to wait until morning," she said to herself. "It will surely be over by morning."

With darkness the steady roar of the winds increased. They howled and shrieked over the prairie like a million coyotes gone crazy. The snow piled up against the windows and blew through every crack.

Geneva fixed a snack for Louis and made another pot of coffee. Time was passing so slowly. Seemed like this day that had started out so beautiful was turning into a nightmare that wouldn't go away.

Finally, Geneva decided to set the lamp in the window. "Daddy will see the light in the window, if he comes. It will help him find his way home."

"Ight in indow for Daddy," repeated Louis as the two of them stood for a moment watching the shadows from the flame dance across the frosty windowpane.

The chilly room brought Geneva back from her troubled self. They'd better go to bed for now. Everything will be better in the morning.

chapter

16

Through The Night

Carl wouldn't give up even as the fierce stormy night surrounded them. "Now listen children, there'll be someone along soon. Now huddle up together. You older ones get on the outside and help keep the little ones warm. Come on, circle around in a huddle and keep shuffling."

So Claude, Rose, Alisha, Crissie, May, Ryan, Erlene and Carl got on the outside and the other thirteen crowded into the middle. There was hardly room to move.

The white night moaned across the ___ less flat land and the storm howled and shrieked ___ freight-train winds continued to rock th ___ shrilly at the cold sleepy children.

"You must not g ___ sleep, you'll freeze. You've got to keep moving." Carl kept repeating and forcing the children to stamp their feet in the darkness.

The older children did try to help Carl encourage and comfort the little ones. The cold and blackness of the night frightened them even more. They begged for their parents and wanted to be home where it was warm and safe.

Ryan was telling the children, "Now listen, my daddy will be out looking for us. Every time there is a storm he goes out on his horse to help somebody. It won't be long."

Sometime around midnight Carl was trying desperately to comfort the stumbling, sobbing children. "I'll let you little ones take turns sleeping. You can only sleep a few minutes."

79

The older children held the smaller ones as Carl rubbed their arms and legs. Rose held her sister, Mabel. Alisha cared for both Leota and Leah. Ryan and Erlene took turns holding their brothers Jon and Joe so they could sleep a little bit. Claude tried to take care of his brothers Earl and Mel. Eva was trying to comfort her brother Larry. Crissie was trying to console Roland and Jimmy while the two sisters, May and Brenda, huddled together. Carl held Mary Louise the rest of the night. Sometimes the children would move about shuffling in the middle trying to get warm.

"Children," he said, "you must not lie down on those benches. You must not let anyone sleep very long."

The benches were tipped up to make more room in the aisle to move around so they weren't comfortable to sit on anyway. Snow had piled up in the back of the bus until they couldn't get the benches down.

May had gone to sleep in spite of all the confusion. Brenda didn't seem to want to move around either. "She'll wake up when help comes," the children were saying. No one was aware she was dying.

Jimmy was getting tired too. When the older ones tried to keep him awake he said, "I'm all right. My daddy is coming." "Daddy is coming," he told them. "My daddy always told me if anything ever happened going to or from school not to be afraid because he'd come and get me."

Friday morning brought new hope of rescue as Carl planned to go for help. He had no idea where they were but he knew he had to have help as the children were going to sleep in spite of all he could do. The storm had not let up. The wind was still blowing and howling with unmerciful force. He couldn't see anything through the wall of blinding snowy whiteness.

"We're up against it, kids," he said. "You older ones don't give up! Wrestle, sing, anything to keep moving. I have to go for help. Be good and pray for my return with help."

As he prepared to leave he took one more look around, "Now, I'm going to get help and we'll have pancakes for breakfast!"

He kissed Mary Louise and gave her a bear hug. She whimpered a little but he patted her on the back and told her, "Be brave until Daddy gets back."

Carl forced a smile on his face, with a cheery "Good-bye" he plunged into the snowdrifts. He had no overshoes and only a light coat for protection against the frigid storm.

There was much confusion now as twenty children fought courageously on their own to obey what Carl had said. Someone got pushed into the front window in a scuffle and it broke. Now snow was piling up in the front of the bus too. They tried to pile the snow up away from them.

"We don't want it to cover the floor," someone warned.

Alicia and Rose thought they saw a car down the road. "We're going to go and see," they said.

So hand in hand they left the bus and walked down the road a little way. "It's gone," Alicia said. "I just know I saw a car!"

"Me too," answered Rose through chattering teeth. "We'd better go back."

The two disappointed girls trudged back to the bus on their frozen feet with no good news for their classmates and families who waited there. Alicia fell into the snow trying to get back into the bus. She couldn't even feel the cold snow. Rose only had on a sweater with extra long sleeves but she pulled them down over her hands trying to keep them warm. She was able to help Alicia back into the bus.

Later the girls thought they caught a glimpse of a building which just might be the schoolhouse. Their hopes soon vanished in the white swirling snow.

The children were becoming exhausted – looking, hoping, shuffling and stumbling. They were really trying to keep each other moving. The older children were trying to rub the smaller ones' arms and legs to comfort them – trying to keep them warm and awake. Now, even the older children were getting weak and suffering from swollen hands and feet. The swelling ripped their shoes apart.

Crissie carried Jimmy's still little body to the back and laid him on the snow. She had done all she could. Roland also had gone to sleep.

"We can't give up now," one of the older boys said sternly.

The terror of the frightened children was slowly giving in to physical and mental exhaustion. They'd had no food and little rest for two days and a night. The extremely low temperatures were slowly defeating the struggling children's fight for survival.

There wasn't much space left as snow had blown in and was piled high in the bus. Finally, they decided to lay their jackets down on top of the snow and pile down together. Carl had been gone a long time now.

Alicia discouragingly told her weary friends with a tremor in her voice, "I don't believe Carl is coming back!"

17

Worried

The wind was still raging as Geneva woke up Friday morning. "Surely it has quit snowing," she thought as she walked to the window. That was only wishful thinking for the snow was still swirling wildly and she knew it was very cold for water had frozen in the kitchen.

She looked at the clock – it was a little before six o'clock. "While Louis is still sleeping I should try to take care of the cattle," she said to herself.

When she went to the door she quickly realized the blinding blizzard still had the prairie paralyzed and helpless. She'd just have to wait. She blew out the lamp to save on fuel and went back to bed until Louis woke up.

Sleep did not come. She was worried and afraid. The storm had come up so suddenly no one was prepared. Hopefully, Carl had made it to the schoolhouse where she knew they would be safe. If only she knew.

Later she built a small fire in the kitchen stove to make a pot of coffee. She had to melt the ice for water. She still wasn't hungry. "I'd better fix some oatmeal for Louis," she thought.

When Louis woke up she fed him. He played quietly like he understood Mama's worry. The waiting and not knowing about the children and her family had created a raging storm in her mind as bad as the fierce storm howling and raging outside. As the fire in the stove began to die down, she knew they'd have to go back to bed for awhile. She would soon be out of corncobs if she didn't use them sparingly. They went back to bed fully dressed.

Geneva was too restless to stay in bed for long so she got up and cleaned the house. She tried to write a letter but just couldn't concentrate. She kept going to the window and trying to see out. She kept thinking she heard someone outside.

Later in the afternoon Mr. Baker and Mr. Jones did come with a team and wagon. Geneva had the door open before they had a chance to knock.

"Did Carl make it back from school?" Mr. Baker asked.

"No, he didn't get back before the storm hit."

"I'm sure they're all at the schoolhouse then," Mr. Baker assured Geneva. "We have food for the children and we're headed for the schoolhouse."

Geneva broke down and began to cry. Mr. Baker tried to comfort her, "Everything will be all right. We'll bring the children back in the wagon. We've got a pile of blankets to wrap them in."

As evening approached the storm abruptly stopped just as it had started. No one returned to let Geneva know if they were all safe. As she looked out across the prairie she could now see a great distance. A feeling of desperation swept over her for Mr. Baker and Mr. Jones had not returned as they had planned.

"I'd better see if I can make it to the barn and take care of the cattle," she said talking to herself. "Now you stay right here in the house," she said to Louis. "Mama has got to go to the barn and feed the cattle."

When she got to the barn there were 31 head of cattle waiting for something to eat. She dug the pitchfork out of the snow and started throwing down hay. The milk pail still hung on the barn wall but she wasn't going to take time to milk as it was still very cold. She dug some boards out of the snow on her way back to the house as the corncobs were almost gone.

When she got back to the house and out of her barn clothes she knew it would soon be dark again. She fixed a bite for Louis to eat and sipped on another cup of coffee. She wasn't hungry — she was worried.

"I've just got to believe that Carl, Mary Louise and the children are all right."

Darkness gradually covered the quiet prairie. Geneva trimmed the lamp, turned it up on high and set it in the window for Carl and Mary Louise. She and the baby had no choice but to go to bed to keep warm, and to hope and pray that everyone was safe and well.

chapter

18

Searching

Mr. Baker and Mr. Jones arrived at the schoolhouse safely in spite of the fierce winds and snow pelting down on them stinging their faces. They could see that the bus wasn't there. Mr. Fry's car was stalled in the schoolyard so they looked for him.

"Where is the bus and the children?" asked Mr. Jones.

"Carl left shortly after he got here yesterday morning. We thought he could get the children home before the storm got bad. The children aren't home?" asked Mr. Fry alarmed.

"No, he didn't get any of the children home. We just went by and talked with Mrs. Miller and he hadn't made it home. She thought they were all here."

"We're going to ~~SAMPLE BOOK~~ kids and the bus!" exclaimed Mr. Baker ~~Not For Resale~~ really worried now as it had been storming ~~two days~~ and one night.

"Which way did he go when he left the schoolhouse?" asked Mr. Jones.

"I really don't know as I was trying to get things ready to leave here myself," answered Mr. Fry. "Miss Emory left before I did and headed south to her place."

It was decided that Mr. Fry would remain at the schoolhouse. Mr. Teague arrived on horseback thinking the kids were there. He joined in the search for the missing children hoping for the best but fearing the worst.

Just before sundown they spotted the stalled bus. The sky was clearing and the storm had ceased almost as suddenly as it had started.

The familiar sounds of galloping and snorting horses and the creaking of the wagon wheels didn't seem to faze the cold and exhausted children who had fought so courageously to stay alive. The wagon came to a halt in front of the bus stalled in a ditch right at the main road. The deathly stillness made them believe they were too late as they plodded through the drifts to the bus.

Some of the children were sitting in the snow near the front of the bus. A pile of coats was in a spot in the aisle and children were dozing off. The smell of stale smoke still lingered in the air.

The fathers wrapped the children in blankets and carried them one by one to the waiting wagon. They worked frantically as they had no time to waste. Three children had already died – one of Mr. Baker's daughters, May; Mr. Jones's only child, Jimmy; and Larry Black. Mr. Teague's children were barely alive.

When Mr. Baker asked about Carl, Claude said, "He left early this morning to get help."

The three worried fathers just looked at each other in despair. Regardless of their losses the men continued to plow through the snow from the bus to the wagon to save the frightened children.

Since the raging blizzard had passed you could see across the prairie to the Hart's farm which was just a-half of a mile away. There would be food and warmth there for the half-frozen and hungry children. The horses raced at full speed as the wagon rocked and reeled with its precious load of critically ill children.

The men carried the children into the house and they were given warm liquids to drink. Mrs. Hart was cooking supper and some of the children devoured the fried potatoes she had cooking on the stove.

Snow, salt and kerosene were rubbed on the children's faces, arms, hands, feet and legs. Some of the children huddled around the stove – others were lying on piles of blankets on the floor nearby.

The word spread quickly and parents were coming to help the children. "We've got to have a doctor," one dad said. "Where is the nearest telephone?"

There were only a few telephones in the area and some of them were out of order. They finally did find a telephone and called for doctors from Holly as well as Tribune, Kansas, to the north.

The doctors fought through ten-foot snowdrifts for many hours to get to the tragic scene – finally arriving about eleven o'clock. The children who had fought so bravely to stay alive were now fighting still another battle – to recover from nearly freezing to death. The battle was lost by two more children before the doctors arrived. In spite of all that was being done, Jon Teague and Mary Louise died after being rescued.

19

The Truth

Geneva heard sounds outside. Quickly she got out of bed. Taking the lamp she rushed to open the door. She just knew that Carl had finally made it home. She glanced up at the clock. It was nearly two o'clock in the morning. When she opened the door there were three neighbor men standing there.

"We've come to see if you are all right," Mr. Collins said through chattering teeth.

"Yes, I'm all right. Do come on in out of this cold," she said stepping aside so they could get inside. "I'm so worried about Carl and the children – are they at the school?"

"No, they weren't at the school. Baker and Mr. Jones located the bus. The ~~SAMPLE BOOK~~ ken to the nearby Hart's farm," Mr. M ~~Not For Resale~~

"Are they all ri ~~Not For Resale~~ of them dead?" she asked expressing her greatest fears.

The men just stared at the floor. Finally, Mr. Newman answered, "They're working with them, they'll be all right."

"The doctors are there now," added Mr. Collins.

"Is Mary Louise dead? Tell me the truth." She couldn't help pressing them for an answer as she sobbed.

"Everything that can be done is being done," Mr. Newman said softly, trying to comfort the worried mother.

"What about Carl?" she asked hopefully as she wiped away her tears.

"He wasn't with the children. They said he left to get help early yesterday morning. I'm sure he found shelter somewhere," Mr. Morris replied as assuredly as he could.

The men never convinced Geneva that Carl was safe. She knew the dangers of this prairie blizzard. She also knew Carl well enough to know if he was all right he would have gone back to the children.

"Please take me to Mary Louise," she pleaded. "I just need to be with her."

Again Mr. Collins insisted, "Everything will be all right. We'll wait until daylight and it will be safer."

Geneva rekindled the fire in the heater so the men could get warm. She started a fire in the kitchen stove to make a pot of coffee. She was worried and afraid. She'd just have to wait a few more hours, but she knew they were holding back the truth.

The men knew she was getting low on fuel. As daylight approached they convinced Geneva to get clothes together for herself and the baby.

"I think it is best for you to go to Carl's parents. You will be warm and not alone," persuaded Mr. Newman looking around the little room and knowing the truth was not good.

"The children will be taken to the hospital as soon as possible," continued Mr. Collins as if trying to convince her that everything would be all right.

As soon as it was light the men bundled up Louis in a blanket and helped Geneva into the wagon. Carl's parents didn't know about the stalled bus until they arrived.

Early Saturday morning two airplanes, an ambulance and several cars arrived to take the critical children, fighting to save their hands and feet, to the hospital in Lamar. They would soon be receiving the medical care they so desperately needed.

In the meantime, Grandpa Miller rode horseback to the Hart's farm. He found out the sad truth – Mary Louise had died.

At daylight a search party was organized to look for Carl. During the day over five hundred volunteers searched every snowdrift in the area for miles around.

Carl was found just before sundown about two and a half miles from the stalled bus. He had sacrificed his life for the children he so desperately wanted to help. He didn't know that his own little daughter and four of her classmates had also died.

The next few days passed like a bad dream to Geneva. She felt like she had been kicked in her heart and floods of tears flowed from her eyes. A feeling of hopelessness and uncertainty from the sudden loss of both Carl and Mary Louise overwhelmed her. So many unanswered questions remained and decisions had to be made.

It was difficult for Geneva to understand how so many people could care about her and the other children and their families. No one knew she only had fifteen cents until payday but she didn't have to worry as the IGA store in Holly sent out groceries and a load of coal.

Over the next few days, floods of help came to Geneva and Louis and all the surviving children and their families. "There are just so many caring people," Geneva told her family as daily there were many cards and thoughtful letters that shared their love and sorrow.

Geneva was told there was school insurance coverage for Carl. This would provide some financial security for her and Louis for the future on the farm. "This is where Carl would want us to be," she told her family and friends.

Carl's brothers and dad were helping with the cattle and chores. Finally, Uncle Ray suggested, "Would you want me to plant the corn and care for the cattle for a share of the crop?"

"I knew it would soon be time to plant the corn," she said. "That would give us feed for the cattle, too, so Louis and I could really stay here on the farm."

Nothing seemed to miss Louis's ears these days as he was staying close to Mama. "Stay at farm?" he asked with all the excitement he could muster.

"Yes, Uncle Ray can help us stay at the farm," she told him as she bent down and gave him a squeeze. He had been so much comfort to her and it was up to her to protect his future.

Now that the cattle and farming would be cared for by Uncle Ray, Geneva decided to spend some time with her family in Oklahoma. She needed time so she could face life again.

"Guess what?" she said to Louis one morning as they were eating a bowl of oatmeal at the little kitchen table. "We're going to go to Grandpa and Grandma Daniels in Oklahoma this week!"

He didn't remember much about Grandpa and Grandma Daniels but he was ready to go if Mama was going somewhere. "Go, wide, Pa!" he exclaimed waving his hands in the air.

"No, we're not going to ride Pa; we're going to see Pa." She even had to chuckle as she explained it to him.

"Goodie, see Pa!" he squealed and clapped his hands. He was ready to go right then but, of course, Mama had packing and things to do before they could leave.

While in Oklahoma a letter came from the White House for Geneva. She sat Louis on her lap and Grandpa and Grandma gathered around as she read the letter from President Herbert Hoover.

> My Dear Mrs. Miller,
>   I have read with deepest sympathy of your husband and daughter's tragic but heroic death. I am sure you will find comfort in the memory of their self-sacrifice.
>   Yours faithfully,
>   Herbert Hoover

Of course they all cried together again as they had done many times before.

Later, the President's aid called and offered her a job at the White House. "I just can't leave my little son," was her final reply. She knew their future was at the farm where she felt close to Carl and Mary Louise.

Two days later Geneva received a check from donations received for her at *The Denver Post* in Denver, Colorado. She couldn't believe her eyes, $2,466.22. It was just too difficult to hold back the tears.

Geneva and Louis returned to the prairie farm and their home with new hope for the future. She felt close to Carl and Mary Louise there with the animals they both loved so much. "This is where Daddy would want us to be," she told Louis when they arrived home.

A few weeks after returning to the farm Uncle Ray took Geneva and Louis to Denver to meet with the people at *The Denver Post*. She wanted to personally acknowledge the gifts given by people everywhere for her benefit. She said, "I am one who knows few words. If I knew them all, I could not express my gratitude to *The Denver Post* and the people of Colorado and many other places for what they have done for me. My heart is too full of thanks to tell about it. I am going back to our farm. I want to make a success of our home for Carl's sake and to have something for our son. I am not afraid of hard work, and I love the country."

Returning to the prairie farm brought much happiness to Geneva in spite of the hardships she had suffered. Much later, Louis learned to ride Prince and take care of him just like Mary Louise. "I take care of Sissie's pony," he told his mama. As he grew older – he did just that!

Epilogue

Carl and Geneva Miller, Mary Louise and Louis moved to the Colorado prairie in the spring of 1930. They lived and farmed north of Holly in the Pleasant Hill Community. Carl was hired as a school bus driver that fall. The blizzard and bus tragedy occurred March 26-27, 1931.

In the little Holly cemetery – with airplanes roaring and showering flowers from the sky – Carl Miller and his little daughter, Mary Louise, were laid to rest on Tuesday, March 31, 1931. Along with them were four other children – Robert Brown, Kenneth Johnson, Louise Stonebraker, and Orlo Untiedt.

Money was raised in various ways by local, state and national organizations to provide funds for all funeral and medical expenses for the families and the survivors.

It would be impossible to recognize all the people who made financial contributions to the Miller family at this time. *The Denver Post's* appeal raised $2,466.22. School insurance coverage also aided the family for several years.

Sympathy and condolences were expressed by strangers throughout the nation including Governor William H. Adams and, from the White House, President Herbert Hoover.

Geneva was offered a job and job training by President Herbert Hoover. She spoke by telephone to his presidential aid. She felt her responsibility was to care for her young son, age two and a half at the time.

At the time of Carl's death, they had fifteen cents until they got the cream check or the school check. The financial help given to Geneva and her young son made it possible for her to return to the farm a few weeks later. "This is what Carl would want," she told family and friends.

Ray Miller, Carl's brother, assisted her with the cattle and farming. Before another winter she did move to Holly rather than spend another winter on the prairie.

Just three weeks after the tragedy, the fifteen survivors and their parents were guests of Frederick G. Bonfils, publisher of *The Denver Post*, for a whole week. They were treated like royalty by scores of merchants and businessmen.

Uniformed chauffeurs transported the children in new Buick cars from the Brown Palace Hotel to the various entertainments and banquets across the city.

All the survivors were presented a solid gold medal by *The Denver Post* in recognition of their courageous survival after being trapped for 32 hours in a raging blizzard. They also visited the capitol in Denver and posed for pictures with Governor Adams.

An enormous amount of parting gifts waited for them in their Santa Fe Pullman cars when it was time to leave. The National Guard ordered five airplanes to escort the children's train out of Denver. On the way home they were cheered by large crowds on the platforms at different stops. Thousands of people cheered as they arrived at Lamar and Holly.

Later, the children traveled on the Missouri Pacific train for another memorable trip to Pueblo, Colorado. They were entertained and honored by *The Star Journal* and other businessmen with banquets, entertainment, gifts and candy. They were also shown the newsreel of their stay at the Maxwell Hospital in Lamar.

All medical expenses were donated by the Charles Maxwell Hospital in Lamar for the survivors. Funeral expenses were also donated by the community for those who lost their lives.

Bryan Untiedt received special honors by the press that included a trip to Washington, DC.

On October 7, 1931 at Holly, Colorado a bus monument dedication was held all day for the unfortunate victims of the tragedy.

In October 1962 a monument was erected at the site of the stalled bus in honor of the brave children and heroic bus driver. For many years only a crude cement block, placed there by the bus driver's brother, marked the spot. It is preserved in front of the larger monument and reads:

"Where The School Bus Stalled In The Blizzard March 26-27, 1931."

The survivors of this tragedy were:

Rosemary Brown
Maxine Brown
Eunice Frost
Leland Frost
Alice Huffaker
Charles Huffaker
Laura Huffaker
Carl Huffaker
Max Huffaker
Lena Huffaker
Clara Smith
Blanche Stonebraker
Bryan Untiedt
Evelyn Untiedt
Ome Untiedt

The families of the twenty courageous children, the bus driver and the surrounding community have continued to live with this tragic saga known as – "The Bus Tragedy of 1931!"

Georgene Pearson

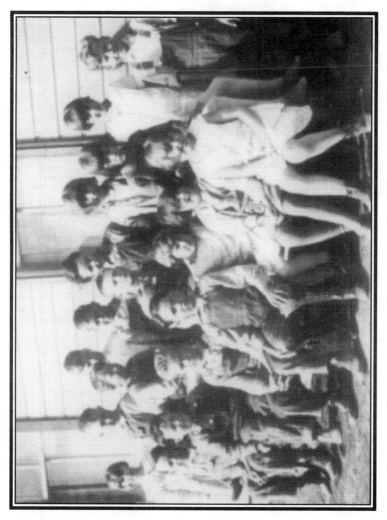

Mary Louise's Class - 1931.

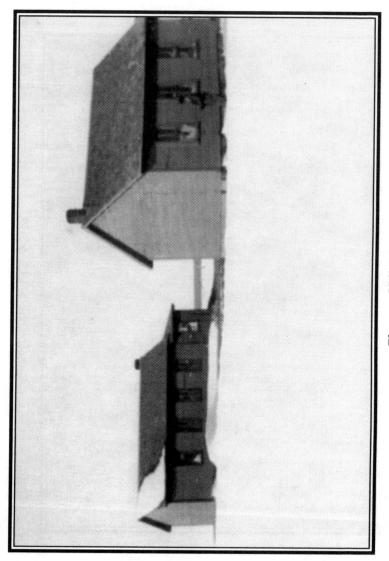

Pleasant Hill Schools.

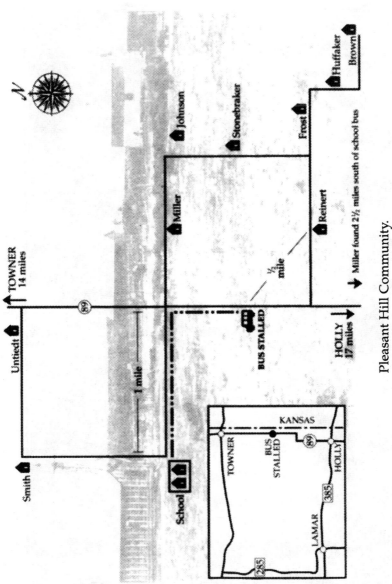

Pleasant Hill Community.

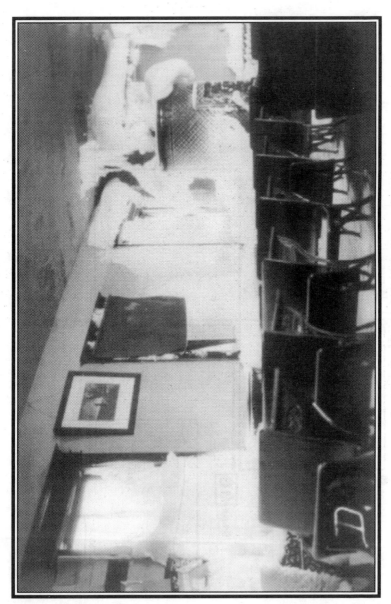

Inside schoolhouse after the blizzard.

Plane and ambulance rescue of children.

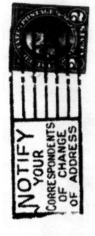

Mrs. Carl Miller,
c/o Box 342,
Duncan, Oklahoma.

THE WHITE HOUSE

THE WHITE HOUSE
WASHINGTON

April 15,1931.

Mrs. Carl Miller,
c/o Box 342,
Duncan, Oklahoma.

My dear Mrs. Miller:

I have read with the deepest
sympathy of your husband and daughter's
tragic but heroic death.   I am sure you
will find comfort in the memory of their
self-sacrifice.

Yours faithfully,

Herbert Hoover

Geneva, Louis and Uncle Ray after the tragedy.

Cemetery Monument - October 1931.

LIST OF SURVIVORS

Rosemary Brown
Maxine Brown
Eunice Frost
Leland Frost
Alice Huffaker
Charles Huffaker
Laura Huffaker
Carl Huffaker
Max Huffaker
Lena Huffaker
Clara Smith
Blanche Stonebraker
Bryan Untiedt
Evelyn Untiedt
Ome Untiedt

1962 monument erected where school bus stalled.
(Original marker in front of new monument.)

Medal given to Geneva by *The Denver Post*.

Geneva and author Georgene Pearson.

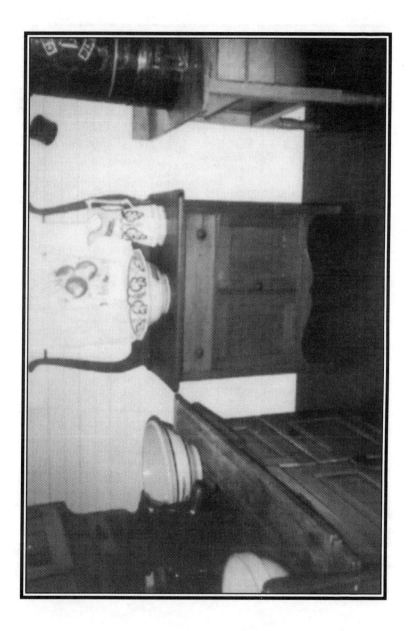

To order additional copies of **(Book Title here)**, complete the information below.

Ship to: (please print)

Name _____

Address _____

City, State, Zip _____

Day phone _____

_____ copies of *(Book Title here)* @ $XX.XX each $ _____

Postage and handling @ $X.XX per book $ _____

(State Abbreviation) residents add XX% tax $ _____

Total amount enclosed $ _____

*Make checks payable to (**Author Name here**)*

Send to: (Author Name here)
(Address here) • (City, State & Zip)

To order additional copies of **(Book Title here)**, complete the information below.

Ship to: (please print)

Name _____

Address _____

City, State, Zip _____

Day phone _____

_____ copies of *(Book Title here)* @ $XX.XX each $ _____

Postage and handling @ $X.XX per book $ _____

(State Abbreviation) residents add XX% tax $ _____

Total amount enclosed $ _____

*Make checks payable to (**Author Name here**)*

Send to: (Author Name here)
(Address here) • (City, State & Zip)